In Search of MOCKINGBIRD

Loretta Ellsworth

Henry Holt and Company ✶ New York

Henry Holt and Company, LLC
Publishers since 1866
175 Fifth Avenue
New York, New York 10010
www.HenryHoltKids.com

Library of Congress Cataloging-in-Publication Data
Ellsworth, Loretta.
In search of Mockingbird / Loretta Ellsworth.—1st ed.
p.   cm.
Summary: On the eve of her sixteenth birthday, Erin receives her
long-dead mother's diary, which reveals that she too revered Harper Lee's
To Kill a Mockingbird and wanted to be a writer, and Erin impulsively
decides to take the Greyhound bus from St. Paul, Minnesota, to Monroeville,
Alabama, to visit the reclusive author.
ISBN 978-0-8050-9695-8
[1. Buses—Fiction. 2. Mothers—Fiction. 3. Authorship—Fiction.
4. Coming of age—Fiction. 5. Diaries—Fiction. 6. Lee, Harper. To kill a
mockingbird—Fiction.] 1. Title.
PZ7.E4783In 2007   [Fic]—dc22   2006018768

First edition—2007
Printed in November 2009 in the United States of America by R.R. Donnelley
& Sons Company, Bloomsburg, Pennsylvania
P1

In Search of

MOCKINGBIRD

For my parents, Gordon and Patricia Mennen—
with love

Sept. 1963

—

I just finished Reading
To Kill a Mockingbird.
It's the best book I've
ever read! I even
wrote to the author.
I asked her, "How
do you know if you
have what it takes
to be a writer?"

In Search of
MOCKINGBIRD

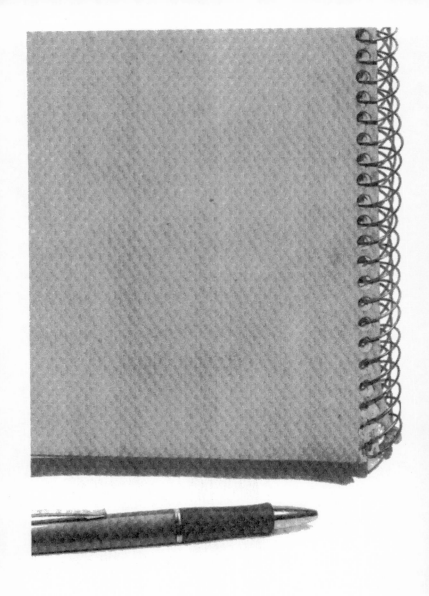

Chapter One

St. Paul, Minnesota
March 13, 1986, 5:30 p.m.

A yellowed paperback
rests in my dusty hands
after I rescued it
from a cardboard box in the attic.
A musty smell lingers in its worn spine.
The dog-eared pages remind me that
a girl, her faded name scribbled
in pencil inside the front cover,
once loved this book, too.

"Erin, get your head out of that book. I have an announcement to make."

Dad's commanding voice is the only thing that could tear me from *To Kill a Mockingbird.* I mark the page with my finger and look up.

Bruce has his arm around Dad's shoulder, a clone except that Bruce is four inches taller. Dark hair, chiseled jaw, straight white teeth, and a smile that proclaims he's comfortable with his good looks. Bruce is studying broadcasting in college, following in Dad's footsteps.

"Listen up," Bruce says. He even talks like Dad.

"What is it?" I ask.

Dad glances at Jeff, who's standing in front of the open refrigerator, gulping down milk straight from the carton.

"Go ahead. I'm listening," he says between swallows. Jeff is Central High's quarterback and an All State basketball player. He's the only senior at school who's been recruited to play basketball for the Minnesota Gophers next year. Who needs manners when you're Dad's pride and joy?

"I just wanted to tell you that Susan and I are getting married." Dad flashes a shy smile and shrugs as if it's no big deal.

"Way to go." Bruce lands a playful punch on Dad's arm.

"That's great. It's about time," Jeff says as he sticks the open milk carton back in the refrigerator.

They all turn and look at me as if I'm supposed to say something, too.

I stare down at the cover of my book. It's been over

a year since I first found *Mockingbird* in the attic. Since then I've read it cover to cover at least six times, some sections more often. I study the penciled notes in the margins where passages are marked and comments made, each pencil mark as important to me as the words in the book itself. I look up and realize they're still staring at me.

"I have to make a phone call," I say as I push back from the table.

Bruce's voice echoes down the hallway behind me. "Don't worry about her, Dad. She's just acting selfish, as usual."

Dad picks the day before my birthday to announce his engagement, and I'm selfish?

"Yeah, she's a freak," Jeff yells. "Just ask anyone at school."

"That's enough." Dad's stern voice fills the room.

I slam the bedroom door behind me. I wish I had a lock on it. Maybe if I'd inherited some of the athletic talent that Jeff and Bruce did, Dad wouldn't shake his head all the time, as if he can't figure out what to do with me.

"It's a classic case of avoidance," Amy tells me on the phone a few minutes later. "You were just a baby when your mom died, and nobody talks about her, that's why you're upset. But it's so romantic that he's remarrying."

Amy's parents sent her to therapy in sixth grade because she seemed depressed. Her therapist always had a sizzling romance novel on her desk. By the end of the year, Amy had developed an addiction to romance novels and had made a new friend, one who liked to read a lot, too. Me.

"You should write about it in your journal," Amy advises. "Get those suppressed feelings out in the open."

Amy says I will be a famous writer someday. I pick up my purple-covered journal and sigh deeply. One book isn't enough to hold all the feelings I have.

It's always been this way: the three of them watching the Vikings football games, playing basketball, wrestling on the living room floor. I'm the geek who carries a journal around with a pencil stuck behind my ear. I write about everything: the twinkle of lightning bugs against a darkening summer sky, a rose wilting beneath a layer of fresh snow, and of course my favorite author, Harper Lee.

"Jeff says I'm a freak," I whimper, waiting for Amy to come to my defense. She doesn't say anything for several seconds, which seems like forever on the phone. I imagine Amy fluffing her puffy bangs and flipping her dark curly hair held back with a banana clip, trying to come up with a believable lie.

"Jeff would be nicer if you didn't act like a lowly sophomore," she finally says. "We're not in junior high anymore."

"You're just taking his side because you have a crush on him," I say. "Believe me, you don't want to date a guy whose nickname is Maniac."

Amy's voice is firm. "Erin, I'm telling you this because I'm your friend. Maybe you should ditch the book."

I glance at my mother's worn paperback. It's the only history I have of my mom. Her favorite book, the one she kept with her all through high school and college and even after she was married. The book in which she wrote little notes, such as "*I love this part,*" and "*Scout's father, Atticus, was more than a man.*"

Dad has a box of old black-and-white photos in his closet; pictures of their wedding, pictures of Mom with Jeff and Bruce when they were little. Not much else to remind us that she existed.

I shake my head. "I'd rather quit school than get rid of *Mockingbird.*"

Her voice rises. "How can you say that? If you

want to be a writer, you have to finish high school. Face it, Erin. Your obsession with that book *is* kinda weird."

The truth at last. My best friend is a traitor. "At least I don't flirt with seniors." My voice is hard.

That does it. She hangs up on me. Jeff is right. I am a freak.

I bury myself in my bed, underneath a pile of blankets. A moment later a small ball of fur jumps on top of me. I grab my gray kitten, Miss Maudie, and snuggle her close to my face. A patch of white circles her nose and one of her eyes. She mews and claws at me to get away.

"You're betraying me, too? Fine." I wrap the blanket around my head, and seconds later she's back on top of me, pawing at the covers. I lift the blanket and she crawls underneath to lie next to my stomach, curling her gray and white specked tail around her.

I rub her head and softly whisper in her ear.

"Someday I'll do it. I'll get on a bus and go to Monroeville, Alabama, and visit my mom's favorite author. Dad told me he might take me there over Christmas break, but then he said he had to work. Now that he's getting married he'll never have time. So I'll go alone.

I'm old enough. I've already planned out the whole trip. Monroeville will be just like I imagine it: white clapboard houses with black shutters and long porches, and magnolia trees in every yard."

Miss Maudie's ear twitches, and she looks up at me. She blinks and looks away, indifferent.

"You don't believe me? I'm not kidding."

I close my eyes and roll back on the bed. I've pictured it in my mind many times. I'll write the whole thirty-plus hours on the bus and fill up my journal. And when I get to Monroeville I'll go see Harper Lee and show her my stories and poems. She'll be there, sitting in her porch swing, waiting to talk to me.

Chapter Two

I'm almost asleep when I hear a soft knock on my bedroom door.

"Can I come in, Erin?" Dad's voice is hesitant. If he's expecting an apology, he's out of luck.

"I don't care."

Dad opens the door. He's holding something down at his side. His face is red, like it is when he hears Amy and me talking about our periods. He hands me a faded white diary held together with a rubber band, the edges discolored and torn.

"I know I should have given you this before." He places the yellowed book in my hand. "I didn't think you were old enough."

He stops and looks embarrassed again.

"What is it?" I ask.

He clears his throat. "It's your mother's diary. She kept it in the nightstand next to the bed. I thought you'd like to have it."

The silver clasp is broken. The word "diary" is etched on the front. The rubber band is dried out, but its impression still worn into the diary. This has been in his bedroom all these years, right next to his bed? Anger swells inside my throat.

"My mom kept a diary? Why didn't you show me this before?" I run into the bathroom, slamming the door so hard the medicine cabinet shakes.

"I'm sorry, Erin." Dad's voice echoes through the door. My heart flip-flops, but I can't answer him. His footsteps sound heavy as he retreats to the den, where I know he'll turn on the TV and disappear for several hours. We just got cable service, and he's already addicted to the sports channel.

I carefully remove the old rubber band around Mom's diary. The book relaxes. It smells like musty pine. *"Kate Kampbell, August 28, 1963—16 years old,"* she'd written on the front page. I recognize the slanted writing from the margins of *Mockingbird*.

I turn sixteen tomorrow. Is that why Dad gave me her diary now?

The porcelain is cold on my back as I plop down on the green shag rug and lean against the tub, propping my feet up on the cabinet. It's a tight fit in the narrow bathroom, but it's the only room where I can lock the door. I spend hours here, so I can have some privacy.

The diary is filled with entries about school and friends and music. I come across an entry that gives me goose bumps.

I just finished reading To Kill a Mockingbird. *It's the best book I've ever read! I even wrote to the author. I asked her, "How do you know if you have what it takes to be a writer?"*

My mom wrote to Harper Lee? Did she write back? I frantically search the diary for a letter, but find nothing. Does Dad know about this?

This is too much. After all these years of not talking about Mom, now he thinks he can just hand me a scrap of her life and make everything okay?

I thumb through the rest of the diary with fascination. At the back of the diary there are three stories, each three or four pages long. I read each one and then go back to where she says she wrote to Harper Lee. My stomach aches, churning like a giant mixer.

Everything is changing. Dad's getting married. Amy will soon have a boyfriend and leave me to wallow alone in tenth grade. Jeff and Bruce are impossible to live with.

"How do you know if you have what it takes to be a writer?"

I run my finger across the words and whisper into the diary, "You never found out." I suddenly know what I have to do. It's like reading my horoscope somewhere and finding a sign.

I retreat to my room and rummage through my underwear drawer. My fingers grasp a wrinkled copy of the Greyhound bus schedule. The bus leaves at seven thirty. Can I make it to the bus station in forty-five minutes? Do I have the guts to do this?

Quickly, I pack a small backpack, gently putting Mom's diary on top. Then I stuff books underneath the covers of my bed and pile teddy bears and quilts across the top. If Dad looks in on me tonight, he won't bother to search under the mess.

I fill Miss Maudie's water bowl to the top and sprinkle extra food in her dish before sneaking out the back door. A carefully placed letter on my desk says it all.

Dear Dad,

I took the money Grandma sent me for my birthday and bought a round-trip ticket to visit someone very special. Please understand—this is something I have to do. I won't talk to strangers and I'll call as often as I can. Don't worry. I'll be back soon. Take care of Miss Maudie.

Love,
Erin

Twenty minutes later, I chain my bike to a rusty pipe outside the bus depot. I'm late. The bus leaves in five minutes. I grab my backpack, take a deep breath, and buy a ticket. I walk outside and find my bus. On the side of it there's a drawing of a greyhound in mid-stride, reminding me that I'm running away. Will Dad come after me? I lied in the letter. He thinks I bought a round-trip ticket, but I only had enough money for one way. And there was another lie. I told him I was coming back.

Chapter Three

Dad's like Atticus.
He's the first to volunteer for a good cause.
I remember hanging on Dad's pant leg at a golf
fund-raiser,
riding in the golf cart,
cheering him on at each hole.
I was only seven years old, and
so proud to have him as my father.
And there's one other way he's like Atticus.
Neither one ever talks about his dead wife.

Since this is my first time on a Greyhound bus I sit alone and try not to choke on the exhaust fumes. A woman across the aisle flashes me a tired smile as she rubs her daughter's back. The girl rests her crimped hair on a makeshift pillow, a large, white teddy bear with black plastic eyes and a red embroidered nose. She looks about ten. She's wearing pink jelly shoes, white lacy socks, and a puffy painted T-shirt with clouds on the back.

The bus pulls out, heading for the interstate. Patches of dirty Minnesota snow splatter up the sides of the bus. The high-pitched whine of the pavement beneath us drowns out the voices of the other passengers.

My worried reflection flickers in the window. I tilt my head to see the tangled mess of hair hastily gathered up into a ponytail. It's the color of dirty sand. If I had my way I'd be a peroxide blonde like Madonna, but Dad won't let me dye my hair.

"It's the same shade as your mother's," he once said, the only time he ever mentioned her.

I try to relax, knowing that they won't find out until morning, when Dad or Jeff will pound on my bedroom door. Jeff will say, "I'm never giving you another ride to school if you don't get your butt out of that bed."

Dad's more subtle. He'll say, "Come on, birthday girl. Wake up. Just because you're sixteen doesn't mean you get to sleep in."

Of course, I'll be hundreds of miles away by then.

The girl across the aisle kicks one foot out. The pink shoe hits the mother's elbow, and the woman lets out a small yelp and massages it.

"Mommy!" The girl whines because her mother has stopped rubbing her back.

I stare at the lacy trim on her ruffled socks. When I was her age I wore Jeff's hand-me-down T-shirts. I should have ended up a real tomboy like Scout. But instead of climbing the tall oak tree in the backyard with my brothers, I curled up underneath it with a pile of books while Jeff and Bruce dropped acorns on my head.

For Christmas, Dad bought me a basketball, an NBA leather one. He just doesn't get it. Even Susan, his soon to be new wife doesn't get it. I guess that makes sense, since she's a volleyball coach. She can talk sports with the best of them. She watches football and reads science fiction.

I open Mom's diary and settle in to spend the next two hours reading. I start over and go through it more carefully this time, cherishing every word as I read about her life in 1963. Partway through a small picture falls out of the middle that I hadn't noticed before. A school picture. *Kate Kampbell—10th grade* is printed on the back. The name doesn't seem to fit the girl with the black-rimmed glasses, teased hair, and uneven smile.

She's a silent memory in our home, like the first years of our lives never happened. When I was ten, I asked Jeff if he remembered her.

"No, but it doesn't matter, because we have Dad," he answered. "It would have been a lot worse if she died after we'd gotten to know her."

"Why would it be worse?"

"You don't miss what you never had." He nodded his head knowingly with all his twelve-year-old wisdom, then picked up the basketball on his way out the door.

But I didn't agree with him. I always missed her even though I never knew her.

A muffled voice interrupts my thoughts as the bus driver speaks into the loudspeaker. "We'll be stopping in Clear Lake, Iowa, for approximately twenty-five minutes. You may depart the bus, but be back on board no later than ten thirty."

Panic rises inside me and I pull out the schedule.

"It's okay," I whisper to my jumpy stomach, "that stop is listed here." I hug my overstuffed backpack to calm the flutters.

A blouse pokes out through the top, and I wonder if I should have packed more than just two outfits. I also brought a pack of cards, colored pencils, and my science textbook. I intend to keep up with my homework, except for algebra, which is a lost cause, and Spanish, because I can't trill my *r*'s, so I figure what's the use?

I turn off the overhead light and stare out the window into the darkness, watching the headlights of the passing cars. The quiet voices of the other passengers have grown louder since the driver's announcement, and I can see from the tops of their heads that several people are shifting restlessly.

The bus pulls into a Burger King parking lot off the interstate in Clear Lake. I look at my watch. It's just after ten. I pull on my winter jacket and get off the bus, my backpack hanging off one shoulder. Even though I'm not really hungry I order French fries and a Coke. I'm too keyed up to think about getting any sleep.

It takes me two minutes to finish the fries. The Coke is for later. I'm the first one back on the bus. I sit in the same spot, an inconspicuous seat right in the middle. It seems to be working. Other than the woman in the seat across the aisle, no one has even made eye contact with me.

I pull out the bus schedule and go over it again, silently repeating the names of our stops: The Boondocks, Iowa, and Sikeston, Missouri. There are two transfers in my trip, one in Kansas City, and one in Montgomery, Alabama, that will take me to Monroeville.

I open my journal. My birthday officially starts in two hours. Drawing a picture of a birthday cake with sixteen candles on top, I scribble *"Happy 16th Birthday, Erin!"*

Two new passengers enter the bus. There are plenty of empty seats; the place is barely half full. My jacket is strung out on the seat next to me in an antisocial attempt to guard my privacy.

A man wearing a painter's cap sits down near the front. A pack of cigarettes hangs out of his coat pocket. They're on the verge of falling, but he doesn't notice.

A woman with golden-brown skin, thick makeup, and curly blond hair draped down past her shoulders picks up my jacket off the seat next to me. I look back at the empty spots behind me, but the woman doesn't take the hint.

"Is it okay if I sit here?" she asks in a nasal voice.

I give her an unenthusiastic nod, stick the jacket behind my back, and return to my journal.

The woman removes her coat and sits down, placing a macramé purse on her lap. She looks at me and flashes a friendly smile. "I'm going to Kansas City. How far you going?"

"Alabama," I say in my most mature-sounding voice. I avoid her eyes as my stomach tightens and I imagine the fries coming up.

"That's a long way for a young girl like you. Do you have relatives there?"

The woman is wearing a low-cut V-neck sweater that ends above skintight black leather pants. Several necklaces dangle down the front of her top. The lines in her neck and the creases in her blue eye shadow remind me of Dad's Aunt Esther, who is sixty years old and still buys Mary Kay cosmetics by the carload.

My hands are perspiring. I'm not good at lying. But she's looking at me expectantly and I have to say something.

"I'm visiting relatives. My grandmother," I add as calmly as I can.

"How sweet. Traveling all that way to visit your grandmother. She's lucky to have a granddaughter like you." The woman buys the story, and I relax a bit. She smiles again, revealing one tooth stained red with lipstick.

"In what part of Alabama does your grandmother live?"

"Monroeville." I lie again, although this time it seems easier.

"I should introduce myself, since we're going to be seatmates for the next five hours. I'm Sedushia Manly."

I have a sudden urge to giggle, but I clear my throat instead.

"That's an unusual name. How do you spell it?"

"S-E-D-U-S-H-I-A. It's not really my given name. It's my stage name. I picked up the last part of the name from a town just north of Mason City where I'm a regular. It has a ring, don't you think?"

"Uh, sure. Are you an actress?"

"Actually, I'm an exotic dancer."

I'm not sure what an exotic dancer is, but I have an idea. I desperately want to ask Sedushia if she is a stripper, but instead I bite down on my lip and think of a less direct question.

"Do exotic dancers wear lots of beautiful costumes?" Her white beaded necklace with plastic orange and lemon slices clashes against two other gaudy necklaces. Silver looped earrings sag from her ears.

"I've got four outfits that I made myself. My favorite is a black lacy two-piece with shiny beads on the fringe. I don't know if you'd call them beautiful, but they're all original." She pulls up on her sweater, as if she's suddenly aware of its low cut.

The driver stands and does a mental count to see if everyone is on board. Sedushia waves at him and looks at my journal. "Are you doing homework? I was thinking of taking an art class at the community college. I've always liked to doodle, but it's hard when you travel as much as I do."

"I'm keeping a journal of my trip." One thing I know about lying: the more truth you weave into your lies, the better off you are.

"A journal. What a great idea. Maybe you'll be a writer when you grow up."

I nod. "I hope so." I read somewhere that if you want to be a writer you have to notice everything. I've already written about the gray plaid seat next to me, the one Sedushia is sitting on, that has a light stain in the center, like dried ice cream.

"I used to have a diary, when I was young,"

Sedushia says. "I remember spending hours writing in it. Don't know where it's gone to now. You be sure and hold on to yours."

"I will." I wonder what a woman named Sedushia who's an exotic dancer would have written in a diary when she was my age. I remember my promise not to talk to strangers unless absolutely necessary. But I'm intrigued and that makes it necessary. Besides, I'm still too wound up to sleep.

My head jerks back as the bus pulls out of the parking lot and heads south onto the interstate, carrying me farther away from my home.

I open my backpack and take out the pack of cards.

"Want to play rummy?"

Chapter Four

"My name's Erin," I offer as I deal the cards.

"That's a pretty name. You look like an Erin. My son, he was definitely a Claude." Sedushia lays down a spade and I pick it up.

"That's a good name." I want to say something nice even if it isn't true. Claude seems almost as bad a name as Sedushia. She lays down another spade and I pick that one up as well.

"Well, he's named after his father and it fits him. His dad and I divorced when he was two years old, and he's lived most of the time with his dad, so I guess it's not surprising he's so much like him. My job took me all over Iowa and Missouri. Since I never learned to drive, I take the bus. It's a comfy ride, but it would be hard with a child. I've played every small

25

town in both states more times than I can count, and a kid needs a stable home."

Sedushia opens her purse and takes out a folded piece of paper, slightly faded. She carefully unfolds it. There's a crayon drawing of a woman with yellow hair down to her waist wearing big black heels. Above the woman are words scribbled in messy red crayon: I MISS YOU MOMMY.

"He drew that for me when he was just six." She smiles at the picture.

"You must miss him, since you travel so much." I lay down a run of spades.

Sedushia shows me her cards and I add up the points. She'd tried to save queens because she thought they were pretty.

"You win," she says with a sigh.

"Oh, my son is all grown up now and works as a car salesman in Kansas City. I did miss him when I traveled, but I tried to see him regularly and spent as much time as I could with him. 'Course, kids don't understand those things when they're young." She closes her eyes and looks down a second, as though remembering something painful, then recovers with a fake smile. "I nicknamed him Boomer because he was such a big thing for his age. Some of his friends still call him that."

"I don't have a nickname. But if I did, I'd want it to be Scout," I add on a whim.

"Scout's an interesting name. Why would you want that?"

I point to *Mockingbird,* which is next to me. "It's the main character in this story."

"I never read it, but I did see the movie years ago. Of course, I had a thing back then for Gregory Peck." Sedushia frowns. "The author's dead now, isn't she?"

"No. She's just very private."

Two thin, penciled eyebrows shoot up in surprise. "I guess when you don't hear about someone for many years you assume they're dead."

"Well, this is the only book of hers that was ever published."

She shakes her head. "Too bad. Someone with so much talent should have kept writing. I have an idea. From now on, I'll call you Scout. How about that?"

"Okay." An alias. I like the idea.

"Well, Scout, if you get tired of my yapping and you want to sleep, just tell me to shut up. I know it's getting late."

"Oh, I'm not tired." I feel like I could stay awake all night, and I haven't even finished my Coke yet. The other passengers are quiet, their bodies twisted in contorted positions as they try to get some sleep. It's cold on the bus, and most of them snuggle underneath their coats, which they're using as blankets. One man is sleeping with a book laid open across his chest, his glasses tilted forward on his nose to the point of almost falling off.

"Are you traveling to Kansas City to visit your son?" I ask Sedushia.

"No, this is work related." Her voice sounds strained. "I have a gig at the Frisco nightclub for six weeks, so I'll be really busy."

She frowns and picks up the cards, shuffling them around in her hands. Somehow, I feel as if I've just insulted her without saying a word, or maybe it's because I don't say anything that she feels offended.

"Maybe you can call Boomer while you're there," I suggest.

She stares at the cards in her hand. "I don't know."

Sedushia flinches and her eyes mist up. She shakes her head. "Let's quit talking about me. I'm boring. I want to hear about you." She puts the deck of cards in one hand. "Have you always wanted to be a writer?"

"Forever. Well, since eighth grade." I want to shift the conversation back to her. Our voices drift throughout the bus, where only the engine noise breaks the quiet of the night. At the moment, everyone seems to be sleeping. A few people wear headphones, but their eyes are closed, so you can't tell if they're sleeping or listening to music.

"Did you always want to be an exotic dancer?" I ask Sedushia.

"Not exactly. First I wanted to be Ginger Rogers and then I wanted to be Grace Kelly. Of course, when you're sixteen you have a lot of dreams and you have no idea how difficult life will be." She pauses, as if she's just realized what she said. Her hand covers her mouth and she looks at me with wide eyes. Then she brings her hand to the side of her face as if that's what she'd meant to do the whole time.

"But I reckon I just wasn't the Ginger Rogers or Grace Kelly type. You, on the other hand, you'll make it as a writer. I can tell. Some people have that assured look about them. A look that says, 'No matter what I set out to do, I'm sure to do it,' as if it's just a matter of fact."

I shake my head.

"Not really," I tell her. "My nickname on the tenth-grade basketball team is Benchwarmer Garven. I'm only on the team because of my brothers. I tried to quit, but Dad wouldn't let me. It doesn't matter to him that I'm only five feet four inches tall and definitely the worst player on the team. I think it's a desperate attempt on his part to find some hereditary link between us that just isn't there." I stop, surprised by all that just came out of my mouth.

Sedushia stares, her mouth half open. She recovers with a small laugh and looks at the cards in her hand as if she hadn't noticed them before. She deals the cards onto the notebook laid out between us.

"That's because you take after your mother." Sedushia nods as though she's an authority on the subject. "I know because Boomer took after his dad and that's why he's so stubborn. He definitely didn't get it from my side of the family."

She winks at me and I smile and pick up my cards.

"I guess you can tell I'm a rambler," she says. "I get started on something and I ramble on and on until somebody tells me to be quiet. And they eventually do. Except for the polite ones like you."

"I like talking to you," I say simply.

Sedushia looks at me above the cards spread out in her hand. "That's about the sweetest thing anybody's ever said to me."

The woman across the aisle taps Sedushia on the

shoulder. "Would you mind lowering your voice? My daughter's trying to sleep."

Sedushia looks across the aisle at the girl curled up on the reclining seat, a small blanket covering her midsection. Her face is half buried in her teddy bear and the scrunched-up part of her face that we can see appears oblivious to the sounds around her.

"What a sweetheart. How old is she?"

"Nine," the woman replies through tight lips as she adjusts the blanket on her daughter.

"Sorry," Sedushia whispers. She points at me. "She couldn't sleep so I'm keeping her company. We'll try to be quieter."

Sedushia turns back to me and rolls her eyes. "Whose turn is it?" she asks in a louder than normal voice.

"It's your turn," I say softly. I don't know if you can get kicked off the bus for talking too loudly, but I don't want any problems. I still have a long way to go.

The bus just left the parking lot in Ames, Iowa. We made a quick stop at The Boondocks, which consisted of a couple of gas stations, a motel, and a diner off the interstate out in the middle of nowhere. Semis lined the parking lot of the diner. Sedushia said it had great food and was always busy, even in the middle of the night. She'd been stuck there once for about twenty-four hours during a winter storm.

It's after midnight and the next stop is Des Moines, scheduled for one a.m.

"When we get to Des Moines, let's get off the bus," Sedushia suggests. "I need to stretch my legs."

I nod. We have a twenty-five-minute layover, and I'm not used to sitting for such a long time.

A rush of excitement mixes with the soda and speeds down to my already nervous stomach. Sedushia is cool, not at all like Susan. Susan acts more like a friend around me than a mom. Her favorite line is "Go for it," which is what she says whenever her team serves at volleyball. It bugs the heck out of me.

I think about my family, sound asleep. I decide to call Dad in the morning before he becomes too worried.

"Once he hears my voice and knows that I'm okay, he'll let me go," I write in my journal between games of rummy.

Then I receive a sign. My pen runs out of ink.

Chapter Five

Ankeny, Iowa
March 14, 1986, 12:30 a.m.

I don't really know what to expect when I find
Harper Lee.
Maybe I just want to tell her how much her book
means to me,
and how much it meant to my mom.
I want to tell her that I wish she'd write another
book,
maybe a sequel to Mockingbird,
so I can see what happened to Scout when she grew
up.
Did she turn out all right?
Will I turn out all right?

The bus hums along through the darkness; the
drone of the engine fills my head. Sedushia has nodded off, the deck of cards still in her hand.

I take out a stack of papers from my backpack, stories I've written that I want to show Harper Lee. Then I read a story from my mother's diary, about a city girl at camp for the first time. She has great descriptions, from the spiderwebs on the windowsills to the stale camp food and the girl's fear of jumping off the dock. I read it again. It's really good. Better than my stories. Mom also has beautiful handwriting. Angular strokes and loops, neatly spaced, as if she took her time on every letter.

"Why did Dad wait so long to show me Mom's diary?" I whisper to the frosty windowpane. My question thaws a small circle of frost and swells up like a balloon.

The driver is listening to a radio talk show. Fragments of words float back, but they're soft and unrecognizable. The bus is quiet except for the occasional passenger strolling back to make a bathroom visit.

I lean my head against the cold window as thoughts overwhelm me.

What am I doing here? I'm not the impulsive type.

Common sense is catching up with me. I've read that Harper Lee values her privacy and doesn't give interviews. What if she shuts the door in my face? What makes me think she'll even talk to me? And most important, if I don't go home, what will I do?

My first thought is to get to Monroeville and then figure it all out. I think of my nightstand at home, full of magazines about writing. I follow their advice most of the time. But sometimes they scare me. "You have to take risks," they say. "You have to find your deepest desires and fears and put them on paper."

I pull on the arms of my sweater, worried that I'm starting to sweat, and then I obsess about how much of a supply of antiperspirant I have left.

The bus slows down and veers off the interstate. One block later, the Greyhound makes a sharp turn into a parking lot, and the passengers begin to stir.

Sedushia snorts and opens her eyes. The cards fall from her hand and land in her lap.

"Hands off, fella," she sneers, then jumps slightly when she sees me.

"Yes, well, we're here. Are you okay? You look flushed."

I stretch and yawn. "I'm fine. Just starting to get sleepy." I stand up and drape my arms through the straps of my backpack, adjusting it onto my shoulders. Sedushia hands me the cards and puts on her coat.

"Aren't you going to wear a coat? It's cold outside."

"No. I'm hot."

"We have to walk two blocks. You sure?"

I nod, wondering what it is that's two blocks away.

The bus depot is located in downtown Des Moines. A group of teenagers with spiked hair stand just inside the door warming their hands underneath a NO LOITERING sign. We walk past them out into the dark. The two long blocks take us past weathered stone buildings. The air feels good at first but soon turns frigid.

After about five minutes, Sedushia heads to the side of one building. Shivering, I follow her. She takes out a key and inserts it into a big red door, then holds the door open for me.

We enter a narrow hallway with fluorescent lighting. Mailboxes are lined in a row along one wall.

"Where are we?" The concrete floor is littered with paper and discarded flyers.

"My place. Come on, I'll show you."

Sedushia leads me up a stairway. We pass a bare

window that looks out at another building less than three feet away.

At the top of the staircase, Sedushia opens a heavy metal door and leads me down a dimly lit hall. She stops in front of another door.

Suddenly, I have second thoughts about Sedushia. I hesitate, trying to think what to do.

"This is it." She fits a key into the door and opens it. The smell of fresh paint leaks out. It's a small apartment. The kitchen and living room are separated by a narrow counter. A fold-down table with two chairs is wedged between the stove and refrigerator, and a pantry shelf built into the wall is covered by a red plaid curtain. Cans of tomato soup and tuna peek out through the fabric.

"I have to use the bathroom," Sedushia says as I linger in the hallway. "I try to avoid using the one at the depot. Plus, I like to check on the place when I'm in town and make sure it hasn't burned down. Come in and make yourself at home."

She disappears, and I walk into the kitchen, leaving the front door open. I check the time on the clock above the stove; it's a cat with a ticking tail whose eyes move back and forth. We have fifteen minutes left before the bus leaves. I shift back and forth on my feet. I can't miss that bus.

I walk into the darkened living room and see pleated curtains and a matching sofa. There's an antique chair in one corner and a wooden curio cabinet in another. In the cabinet are pictures of a smiling round boy with black curly hair. On another shelf there's a black-and-white photo of a younger Sedushia in a sequined costume and tap shoes. A sash across the front of her dress reads "Miss Tap Award." She wears a lopsided crown, and a wide smile lights up her face.

A yellow telephone sits on a small end table. I stare at it for about ten seconds, contemplating calling Dad. Another look at the ticking clock convinces me not to wake him.

A moment later Sedushia returns.

"You're a great decorator," I tell her as she approaches.

"Thanks, but I have a confession." She opens a drawer in the kitchen and pulls out *Good Housekeeping* magazine. Her hands flip to a creased page, which looks identical to her living room. "I sit at night and dream of having these rooms." She turns to another picture of a luxurious bedroom. "This is next, when I get the money." She puts the magazine away and picks up her purse.

"Are those pictures of your son?" I nod toward the cabinet.

"Yeah. That's Boomer. Wasn't he a chunky little one? I don't have any recent photos, but I hear he's a hefty guy."

She bites down on her lip. "I mean, he's still big." She pauses a long moment, twisting the straps of her purse between her fingers. The cat's tail ticks in the uncomfortable silence.

Sedushia looks at me. "You can probably guess that I don't see him much. I haven't seen him on a regular basis since he was twelve. A few visits every now and then, visits that weren't welcomed."

"I'm sorry," I mutter softly.

She waves her hand away like it doesn't matter, but her voice sounds forced. "Water under the bridge. In my line of work I expect as much. Boomer's father didn't help any. He never supported me."

"He wanted you to quit dancing?" I ask quietly.

She nods. "Claude wanted me to give up something that gave me joy. I've never been one to apologize for my love of dancing. A few years ago I danced with a woman from Taiwan. Did you know that in Taiwan exotic dancers perform at funerals, and even some weddings? It's classier than it sounds, and the money can be great, once you get a few regular customers and learn to pole dance."

I'm intrigued. This certainly wasn't in the career opportunity brochure at Central High.

"I've been on my own since I was your age. I met Claude at a nightclub where I danced. He was a regular. I kept dancing till I got pregnant with Boomer. Then we decided to get married and I quit for a few years." She sighs. "I tried a regular job. I worked in the shoe department at Sears for a while, but I couldn't take the smelly feet and early-morning hours. I wanted to dance again. There's more to it than that, but the short version is that Claude divorced me and kept Boomer."

I point at the photo of her. "You used to tap dance?"

Sedushia nods. "We all start out with high hopes. I guess that's as close to Ginger Rogers as I'll ever get," she says with a smirk. "But you gotta do what you gotta do. Right? Come on." She moves toward the door. "We don't want to miss that bus."

We run the two blocks back to the depot, Sedushia keeping up with me the whole time, even in heels.

The bus is full. Most of the people stayed and slept.

We settle into our seats as the bus turns onto the interstate. It's one thirty in the morning and I'm starting to get what I call the sleep headache, the kind that buries itself just below the surface and nags at you like an overbearing itch that won't go away. I hadn't thought to bring Tylenol. I take out *Mockingbird*. Sometimes reading helps me feel better. But after several minutes I press my fingertips into my temple.

"Have a headache?" Sedushia asks.

I nod.

"Here." Sedushia opens her purse, which could pass for a traveling pharmacy. She pulls out six bottles filled with vitamins. Then she places eight prescription containers on her lap. Finally, she opens a huge bottle of Tylenol and hands me two tablets.

"Thanks." I swirl them in my mouth with watered-down Coke.

She gathers up the drugs and sticks them back in her purse.

"Do you use all of those?"

Sedushia shrugs. "At one time or another." She lets out a small laugh. "I'm not as limber as I used to be. Dancing is hard on a body that's my age."

"You don't look that old," I say with too much enthusiasm, a half-truth that doesn't quite come off sounding natural.

Sedushia smiles in the dim light of the bus. "I can top that one. You don't look like a runaway."

Chapter Six

"Don't worry, Scout." Sedushia pats my arm. "I'm not going to turn you in or anything. Who would I talk to if I did?"

But I am worried. What if someone heard her? I look around at the sleeping passengers.

What a dope I'd been to think I had her fooled this whole time. I slump over, defeated and embarrassed. "How did you know?"

"I'm not in line for the mother of the year award, but even I know it's strange to send a kid on a trip in the middle of the night, especially with all the stops we make. Besides, I ran away myself at sixteen. I know the look."

I straighten up. "What look?"

"The look of someone who's left everything

43

behind. I've seen it lots of times on the bus. Some of them are way younger than you. Lord knows you're old enough to know what you're doing. At least you *think* you are."

"I'm not sure about that anymore." My eyes feel moist.

"Does it have to do with your mom?"

"My mom?" It seems like Sedushia knows so much about me even though I've told her so little.

"It's just that you haven't mentioned her at all. I've heard you talk about your dad. But not your mom. You're not close to your mom, are you?"

"Not really," I confess. "My parents aren't together."

"Oh." She nods as if she understands.

I feel the sudden need to come clean with the truth. "Actually, my mom is dead and my dad is getting remarried."

"Gracious me. I'm so sorry." Sedushia puts her arm around me.

"It's okay. I don't remember her. She died when I was a baby."

"And you have a problem with your dad getting remarried?"

I shrug. "No. Well, maybe."

Sedushia sighs. "I can relate to that. My ex remarried when Boomer was just eight. I get compared to Joyce all the time." Sedushia leans over and says in a nasal voice, "She has a respectable job. She's a bank teller."

"Susan is okay," I add quickly. "My dad has been dating her for three years, so it's not a big shock or anything. My brothers love her, and I think she's nice. She's just not . . . my mom."

"Hmm." Sedushia thinks for moment. "Have you talked to your dad about any of this?"

"No."

"What about grandparents? Can you talk to them?"

"My mom was from Ohio. She didn't have any brothers or sisters, and we didn't see my grandparents much. My grandma died when I was five and my grandpa died two years later. My dad's relatives live in Chicago. They don't talk about my mom, probably because it makes my dad sad. I have to sort things out on my own."

"And where are you going to do that?"

I hug my book tightly as more truth spills out. "Monroeville, Alabama. Except I don't have a grand-mother there. I'm going to meet Harper Lee."

"That author? Do you know her?"

"Not exactly. I feel like I know her. Have you ever

done something on the spur of the moment? Something crazy and radical?"

Sedushia laughs, and the woman across the aisle moves around a bit. Sedushia doesn't seem to notice and laughs again. "Erin, you just pegged my whole life."

"So you're not going to try to talk me out of it or anything like that?"

"Would it do any good?"

I look down at my book before answering. "No." My voice is determined.

Sedushia nods knowingly. "But you need to hear something I failed to learn when I ran away."

"What's that?"

"It's never too late." She enunciates each word as if she's talking to someone who reads lips.

I nod as if I understand, but I don't really.

Sedushia reaches over. Her bright red fingernails tightly grip my hand. "It's a hard lesson. I never did get the knack of it."

My hand feels numb. "If it's never too late, then why don't you call your son?"

"That's not what I meant. I meant it's never too late to go home."

"But it's the same thing," I insist.

Sedushia's face twists into a smile. "You're awfully smart for a kid. You're right. But it's been ten years since I've seen him. And like I said, I never did get the knack of that lesson."

I rub my eyes, stifling a yawn. "You're too proud," I state as though it's a fact.

"No, it's not that." She shakes her head and her voice shakes as well. "You can't call someone after ten years. I haven't seen him since he was fifteen, after he told me he was embarrassed to have me as his mother. What would I say to him now? And what good would it do? He wanted me out of his life."

"But he was just a kid. Maybe he's changed his mind."

"Maybe," she says, a glimmer of hope in her voice.

"You should see him. What've you got to lose?"

"Oh, I have lots to lose. You're not the only one with an imagination, Scout." She fidgets with the zipper of her coat and looks out the window. "I have some dreams left, you see. That one day my son will come and find me. Sometimes, in my dreams, he invites me to live with him and his family. And of course I pack up and move in with them and spend my days playing with the grandkids. Then there's the dream where he's looking for me and we see each other on the street and we hug and the past is suddenly wiped away." She stops and presses her hands together. "So if I visited him at his house in Kansas City and he told me that he hates me and never wants to see me, how would I be able to keep on dreaming those dreams? I'd have nothing left."

"I hadn't thought of that." I look down at my book. I wonder if there's something in here that applies to Sedushia's problem.

In *Mockingbird,* Scout's father, Atticus, is an attorney who defends a black man accused of raping a white woman in the 1930s, even though he knows the case is lost before it even begins. Atticus feels that it's the right thing to do.

I hesitate. It isn't like me to push my way into someone else's problems.

Sedushia is wringing her hands. I instinctively reach over and put my hand on hers.

"Maybe there's a way you can talk to him without losing those dreams."

Sedushia raises her eyebrows.

I think of Scout and it suddenly comes to me. The book rolls between my knees, and the cover glimmers in the faint light of the moon.

"Did I tell you I believe in signs?"

Chapter Seven

Writing isn't supposed to be easy.
Harper Lee spent two and a half years
rewriting Mockingbird.
And now, while reading one of Mom's stories,
I see the pain of crossed-out words
replaced by other hard-thought ones
and I understand exactly how she felt.

For the next half hour I work on my plan. It isn't a carefully thought-out plan, but it's the middle of the night. At this hour, just the fact that I can still think is inspiring.

I tear out a piece of paper to make notes, leaning over so I can ask Sedushia questions without waking the other passengers. The whir of the engine and the

49

swish of passing cars echo through the dim shadows of the bus.

"We arrive in Kansas City at four fifty-five a.m., and I have a two hour and twenty minute layover before the bus leaves again. Do you know where your son lives?"

Sedushia shrugs, then nods her head. "Actually, I've been past his house a couple of times. He got married last year and lives on the south side of town." She adds, "'Course, I wasn't even invited to the wedding."

"How far is his place from the bus depot?"

She bites down on her lip. "Oh, I don't know. Maybe a half-hour drive."

"Great. That gives us plenty of time. Figure one hour for driving time and we still have over an hour left."

"An hour for what?"

"To talk to Boomer."

Sedushia brings her hand to her throat and gasps. "Lord, we can't go to his house at that time of the morning. We'll be there at five thirty."

"Then we'll be sure to catch him at home."

"But we'll wake him up. No, Boomer was always

moody in the morning. I don't think that's a good idea."

I pat her hand. "It's okay, Sedushia. You won't be waking him up. You'll be in the cab."

She looks at me, puzzled.

"Can I borrow that picture," I ask, "the one Boomer drew for you when he was six?"

She opens her purse and carefully takes out the drawing. "You won't lose it, will you?"

"Of course not," I assure her. I point at my book. "In *Mockingbird*, someone leaves gifts for Scout in a tree hole. At first she thinks it's some kind of magic; later she realizes her neighbor is leaving the gifts." I point to the picture. "I'm going to leave this in Boomer's door with a note. After he's had a moment to look at the picture, I'll talk to him. Then I'll come back to the cab and talk to you."

Sedushia looks at the drawing and nods her head. "I see what you're doing. You're going to be my bouncer, my go-between."

I open a notebook, searching for an empty sheet of paper. "Well, let's just say that I'm making sure you keep your dreams intact."

"But what will the note say?"

I narrow my eyes, willing my brain to work despite a dull headache. "I thought I'd borrow an idea from *Mockingbird.* Something like how you never really know a person until you stand in his shoes and walk around in them. How that's true for mothers as well."

Sedushia looks in the air as if the words are written in front of her. She turns to face me and her eyes are soft. "I like it." She puts her hand on my arm. "But Scout, don't feel bad if it doesn't work. I mean, I wouldn't get your hopes up."

I rip out a sheet of paper and get to work.

Sedushia looks around the quiet bus. "You know, I've been riding the bus for twenty-three years. Used to be that people cared enough to talk to one another. Sometimes I'd have two men fighting over who'd sit next to me. Even the women who objected to my profession talked to me, if just to tell me I was a victim of male chauvinism or to push their bookmarks printed with Bible verses. But the last five years have been different. Sometimes I ride for two days without anybody saying a word to me."

She flashes a quick smile. " 'Course, I could tell from the start that you were different. I guess I'm going the roundabout way of saying thank you."

My family doesn't usually go for sentimental slop, as Bruce would call it, but I smile back and do what my social studies teacher says people lack the ability to do today. I accept her thanks and say, "You're welcome."

Then I flatten the piece of paper against my book and use a green pencil because I read in Amy's teeny-bopper magazine that green is a healing color and I figure we need all the help we can get.

I print *Dear Boomer* at the top of the page and something strange happens to me inside. I look at the words and, for the first time in my life, I feel like a writer.

Dear Boomer,

You can't possibly know how much I've missed you. I've made a lot of mistakes. No excuses. But you never really know a person until you walk in his shoes.

I only ask that you talk to me and give me a chance to explain.

Most sincerely,
Mom

Chapter Eight

I've been reading my mother's diary.
Her uncensored thoughts,
how she loved the Beatles
and cried when JFK died.
But it only covers one year.
What happened after that?
Why did she stop writing?

"Kansas City is warmer," Sedushia informs me. "At least the weather is," she clarifies as a man bumps into her then hurries off the bus without so much as a "sorry."

But it feels cold when we get off the bus. It's still dark out. The station is bustling with people, most of them boarding another bus farther down. Several people linger in the lighted waiting area, their eyes fixed on a TV above them where the Weather Channel is playing. The number forty-seven flashes above the weatherman's head. "About average for mid-March." His voice drifts out the open door. We wait for the driver to take Sedushia's suitcase off the bus, which is a slow process because he's taking everyone's luggage off. The passengers who are traveling on have to transfer to a different bus that hasn't arrived yet. I make a note of the new bus number.

Maybe it's because I'm with Sedushia that I feel safe standing here. A seedy character dressed in a fur coat and wearing dark glasses stands next to the luggage rack. A guy with orange hair smokes a cigarette behind me. There are several Spanish-speaking people huddled in a group. I can't understand what they're saying, except for the occasional "*sí.*" I remember a sign posted in my Spanish classroom that states, "Everyone smiles in the same language."

I think of Monroeville, Alabama, advertised as being a friendly place, but protective of their town celebrity, Harper Lee. How will they greet me?

I've read all about Harper Lee. Old interviews. Essays published in *McCall's*. Newspaper and magazine articles that can't decide if Miss Lee has been secretly writing and has half-written manuscripts lying around her house, or if she's been publishing books under a different name. Rumors abound. They say her childhood friend Truman Capote is the real author of *Mockingbird.* They say she's reclusive. They say she died years ago. They all want to know, Where has she been and what has she been doing for the last twenty-five years? Not unlike the questions Boomer will soon be asking Sedushia.

We hail a cab, and Sedushia gives the driver the address. Two minutes later, we're headed south in a gray Ford Escort, bouncing along on a ripped vinyl seat. I stare at the numbers spinning by on the meter perched on the dash. It's the first time I've been in a taxi.

"To the west, three blocks down, is the Tropica Calor," Sedushia says as she points out the window. "I've worked there a lot. And the best Italian restaurant in town is just two blocks over yonder. They have an antipasto dish that would make your mouth water."

For the next fifteen minutes she points in every direction and talks a mile a minute. I don't know if that's her way of staying calm, but it drives me nuts.

"There's a delicious bakery on the way. I wonder if

it's open yet," she says, then leans forward in her seat. "Do you know if the Pieta Bakery's open?"

"No, ma'am." The driver doesn't turn around.

She looks at me. "Maybe we should stop and get something to eat first."

I shake my head. "There isn't enough time."

"But you'll get hungry on the bus."

"I'm not hungry, Sedushia."

"Maybe not now, but you will be later."

"I'm fine." I know she's stalling, but we don't have time to waste. It's almost six o'clock, and we're behind schedule. Plus, I have no idea how much time to allow for a reunion, if there is one. I suspect those things take a while. And we'll be fighting rush-hour traffic on the way back.

"Don't you think you should call your dad? He's probably sick with worry."

"I'll call him later."

"Take the next exit," Sedushia tells the driver, and I open my mouth to object.

"It's a shortcut to Boomer's house," she explains.

The driver turns onto a one-way street for several blocks before Sedushia guides him past three more turns into a modest neighborhood of older homes.

Stately, tall oaks line the roadway, and there's a quiet beauty as daybreak lightens the tops of the trees. Sedushia interrupts the peaceful scene with a high-pitched scream.

"Stop! It's there." She points up the street to a white house with black trim and a screened porch that's two houses away. Her hands are in constant motion out of nervousness. My hands are shaking, too.

"All right," I croak as a sudden chill creeps up my spine. After several seconds spent searching for the letter I wrote—it is sitting on my lap—I take Boomer's picture and tuck it inside the letter.

"You stay here. And don't worry. It'll be fine," I say with a confidence I don't feel.

She nods. "Good luck."

I get out of the cab and walk toward the house like a condemned prisoner approaching the guillotine.

I look back at Sedushia and she waves.

"I can do this."

I repeat that phrase several times in my head, but a different image pops up, the scene from *Mockingbird* when the kids talk of knocking on the door of Boo Radley's house, but they're afraid of getting killed. I shake off the image, but I'm shivering through my heavy jacket.

The horizon is getting lighter. I've been awake for twenty-four hours now. I should be exhausted, but instead my heart races and I have to take even steps to keep from breaking into a run. Are my eyes bloodshot? And my hair! I quickly run my fingers through my ponytail.

Two large evergreens stand in front of the house. I wait for a few long seconds before going up the steps, pushing open the screen door, and stepping inside a cluttered porch. There are several white plastic chairs covered with dust, two bicycles, a Christmas wreath, and four cardboard boxes piled on top of each other.

A wooden door separates the porch from the house. I don't turn the knob, because I figure it's locked and I shouldn't have come this far to begin with.

Now, where to put the letter? I try sliding it in the door, but it doesn't fit. It doesn't work underneath the door, either. Besides, Boomer might not look down when he answers the door. I don't have any tape with me or I'd tape it to the door. I'm still trying to figure out what to do when there's a loud thud.

I spin around. A newspaper boy rides past on a bicycle. The folded-up newspaper had hit the screen of the porch and landed on the sidewalk below.

I step back outside and pick up the newspaper, rolled up and secured with a rubber band. This is my answer. Sticking the letter inside the rubber band next to the newspaper, I set it back on the ground. I tiptoe inside and take a big breath.

"Here goes nothing." I pound on the door several times. Then I run out the door, down the steps, and around the side of the house.

Still nothing. Finally, a large man steps out of the house. He's wearing boxer shorts and a sweatshirt. His feet are bare and he's tiptoeing back and forth on the cold cement. His unshaven round face moves from side to side. Short, curly black hair is matted on one side of his head and sticking up on the other side.

This is Boomer? What a loser!

Boomer bends down with some effort and picks up the newspaper, then takes one more look around before he heads back into the house. Now all I have to do is wait. Once he reads the letter, he'll surely come back out, hopefully with more clothes on.

I wait several minutes. Still no Boomer. Has he

noticed the letter yet? My dad always reads the newspaper first thing in the morning, but some people just bring it in and stick it on the counter. What if Boomer takes the paper to work to read? What if he takes a shower before he reads the paper? I'm not sure we have time to wait for Boomer to take a shower. We barely have time for him to get dressed.

I'm just wondering whether the newspaper idea was stupid, when a woman across the street opens the front door and lets her huge black dog outside. The dog sniffs around for a moment, then pees, then sniffs some more. Suddenly, he looks up and eyes me across the street. The dog lets out a monstrous bark as he runs straight toward me. My brothers always say, "Never run away from a dog if you're scared." So I scream and run around to the back of the house. When I look back, the dog is right behind me and he doesn't look friendly. I keep running all the way around to the front of the house and do the only thing I can think of. I run inside the porch and slam the door behind me. The dog stands at the screen and barks loudly.

"Down, Fido," I say through the screen.

The sound of approaching footsteps startles me.

The door behind me opens and I turn to look. Boomer is there, his head almost touching the top of the doorway. His dark eyes are bulging and his mouth is open. He's monstrous up close. I look back at Fido, still barking through the screen door. Maybe I should have taken my chances with the dog. Odds are, they both bite.

Chapter Nine

Boomer's House
March 14, 1986, 6:00 a.m.

"That dog is dangerous!" I stammer, shrinking back and pointing at the barking monster on the other side of the screen door.

Boomer pushes past me and yells at the mutt. "Go home, Duke. Get along now."

The dog takes one last hungry look at me and crosses the street, where at the same time his unsuspecting owner opens the front door and scuttles Duke back inside, unaware of his near-miss assault.

Boomer turns to face me, and his assault is worse.

"Who the hell are you?"

I cringe but attempt a soft smile. "I'm Erin." Boomer is wearing a pair of sweatpants and a faded gray T-shirt with KANSAS CITY ROYALS printed on the front. "I'm a friend of your mother's," I add.

"My mother?" He looks confused and I suspect he hasn't seen the paper yet.

"There's a note. It's in your newspaper," I explain. I want to leave, to run out the door and disappear into the bushes until this whole day has passed. But Sedushia is waiting in the cab, hoping for Boomer to say some kind word, even though I can tell that nothing of the sort is ever going to happen. Sedushia said that Boomer sells cars. I wonder if he scares his customers into buying them.

"Wait here," he yells, then disappears into the house. I stare at the white plastic chairs covered with dust. What will I say to Sedushia when Boomer kicks me out?

"Reality Bites" is carved on one of the stalls in the girls' bathroom at my high school, and right now it seems so true. I don't have a mother and Boomer doesn't want his. I realize that today is my birthday, that it's been my birthday since midnight and I haven't thought about it much till now. I was born at ten a.m., though, so I'm not officially sixteen yet.

A folded-up army cot rests near the window, and I'm reminded of my four-poster bed at home.

Boomer opens the door and comes back out. He's carrying the note and picture.

"How do you know my mother?" he barks.

"I met her on the bus." I look down at the floor. That sounds so lame.

He shakes his head. "She sent a kid this time?"

This time? There were others? My mouth drops open. Boomer nods.

"About once a year she tries to contact me. Usually gets some poor sucker to call me on the phone and ask if I want to talk to her. Never had anyone come to my house, though. And she never used a kid before."

"I offered," I say defensively. "She's here. She's in a cab down the street."

Boomer peeks out the screen as if he doesn't believe me.

"She didn't know if you'd want to see her," I explain, feeling stupid. The whole idea now seems pathetic.

He quickly scribbles something on the note, then hands the picture and note to me. "Tell her to stop trying. Tell her it's too late for a reunion."

I open the screen door. I'll have to tell her the latest attempt failed as well. But then I think of *Mockingbird*, of how Scout didn't give up when a mob of men surrounded the jail and her father, how she kept talking to them until she'd broken the spell of resistance and made them see reason. I stop and spin back around. "Why is it too late?"

He waves me away. His lip curls up in the same way as Sedushia's.

"You wouldn't understand, kid."

I wouldn't understand? Like I don't have issues of my own? I stand up tall and my voice is strong. "Sedushia told me that she made some bad choices. But she's your mom. You should give her another chance."

Boomer's dark eyes narrow into tiny slits. "Another chance? She's gone for ten years and then all I get is a few phone calls from strangers wanting to know if I'll see her. She doesn't have the guts to call me herself and now she wants to waltz back into my life. I don't even know her anymore."

I dig my heels into the floor and find an even louder voice. "That's because you pushed her away. She only stopped seeing you because you said you were ashamed of her."

"My mother's a stripper."

"My mother is dead."

Boomer takes a step back. "Sorry," he mutters. He looks around for a moment as if reconsidering.

"She's waiting in the cab," I add again.

Boomer lets out a heavy sigh.

"I have to get ready for work," he announces.

"Did you ever wonder why she uses other people instead of calling you herself? Maybe it's because she's afraid of rejection," I say as I open the screen door on my way out.

"Do you have her phone number?"

I close the door and turn around, surprised.

Boomer puts his hands up and quickly adds, "No guarantees."

A true car salesman.

"Sorry. I don't have her number, but she's performing at the Frisco nightclub for six weeks. You can call her there."

"Maybe I can catch her act," Boomer says sarcastically.

"Maybe you can give her a chance," I snap at him. "She's not asking for anything more."

He puts his hands up in defeat. "Sorry, kid. You're right. I guess it wouldn't hurt to talk to her. Even though she wasn't much of a mother."

He sticks out his palm. "Let me see that note again."

I hand him the note, and he flattens it up against the door and scribbles something on it that I can't read because his head is in the way. Then he folds the note in half and hands it back to me.

"That picture got to me. Can't believe she saved it all those years." He shakes his head in disbelief and his voice sounds almost pleasant.

I nod in appreciation, thinking that Boomer isn't quite the son Sedushia expected.

"Hey, kid," he says as I leave, "watch out for the Great Dane next door." I look back, and he has a smirk on his face. I wonder if Boomer is worth the effort.

Chapter Ten

The Burbs of Kansas City
March 14, 1986, 7:00 a.m.

Unspoken lies are the worst kind.
Scout said she was young when her mother died,
and she never missed her presence.
I was preoccupied with my mother at an early age,
like a memory long gone that I yearned for.
I think Dad missed her, too,
even though he didn't say that he did.
"Was Mommy pretty? Did Mommy have long
hair?"
"Yes." "No." Short answers masked in sadness.
Did I say something wrong?
Finally, I stopped asking.

"I hope we get back in time," Sedushia worries out loud, leaning forward as if to make the taxi move faster.

"It's not far," the driver replies, and he gives the car a boost of gas as he rounds a corner. I nearly do a body slam into the side of the car but catch myself on the rip in the seat.

Sedushia stares at the note, her jaw clenched in tense determination. I'm not sure if it's the note, which she hasn't read yet, or the race back to the depot that's causing her anxiety. Maybe it's both.

I know I should be worried, too, but I'm exhausted. If I miss the bus, I plan on sleeping at the terminal. After facing a killer dog and Boomer, nothing at the station could scare me. I rest my head on the back of the seat, waiting for Sedushia to read the note. I hope Boomer was kind.

"Read it, Sedushia," I implore her. "There's no way I'm getting out of this cab until I find out what he wrote."

She cradles the paper in her hand like a delicate flower. Her eyes widen and her hands tremble as she opens the note. I'm holding on to my seat as the cab rushes another corner doing almost fifty miles per hour.

Sedushia mouths the words silently and her expression changes to one of joy. "It's good!" she shrieks, then grabs my arm and holds on to it as she reads.

"I will meet you for dinner. Call me at work at the number below to set up a time and place. Boomer."

She squeezes my arm. "I'm going to see my baby," she whispers.

I almost tell her not to expect Boomer to pay for dinner. Instead I just smile through the pain of her sharp nails.

The bus terminal is up ahead. Our timing was close, but it was worth the hassle to see the look on Sedushia's face when she read the note, and to know that Boomer is giving her a second chance.

Sedushia pats my arm. "I knew you could do it, Scout."

"Ah, yes," I reply as I think of the other unsuccessful pawns before me. I don't mention that I know there were others who tried. It could have been a setup this whole time, her sitting next to me, the instant bond she said she felt. I should be mad, but I feel close to her somehow. I figure if she gets her son back, it doesn't matter. She had enough guts to keep trying.

"Do you know which bus you're supposed to be on?" Sedushia asks as the cab pulls up to the curb in front of the bus depot. It's seven ten and I have less than five minutes to get on board.

"I think so." I check my ticket, then jump out and turn to face her.

She hangs on to the door and shrugs her shoulders as she flashes me a wistful look. We both stand there for a long moment, searching for words. Finally, I pull out a scrap of notebook paper and scribble my name, address, and phone number on it. She closes her hand around it and reaches over and gives me a quick hug; her chunky earrings press into my face. She smells like drugstore perfume, the kind that comes in a package with matching powder.

"Don't give up your dream. You have to make it to Alabama and find what you're looking for," she whispers in my ear.

I hug her back. "Thanks."

"And don't forget to call your dad and let him know you're all right."

"I will. Good luck with Boomer."

Her smile crinkles the corners of her mouth. "I'll need lots of luck."

I turn and run for the bus. It's unsatisfying to leave her so suddenly, like putting down a book halfway through, not knowing the end.

A man and his daughter walk by, and I wish I had time to call Dad. But I want to make it to Alabama, so I dash past the phones as I hurry in the opposite direction.

The bus driver is looking to pull out when I run up and slam my fist against the door. He opens it and I thrust my ticket at him.

The man puts out his hand to block me.

"You don't have any luggage, do you?" he asks loudly.

"No."

He lets me on, but the passengers stare at me with pinched faces. A woman looks at her watch and shakes her head in disgust. I'm definitely sitting alone.

I find an empty seat and open *Mockingbird* to one of my favorite chapters, the one where the kids sneak into Boo Radley's yard at night, eager for adventure. They get shot at and barely escape as Scout's brother loses his pants while crawling underneath a ragged fence.

I'd felt the same rush of fear and excitement this morning, running from Duke and facing up to Boomer. More thrills than I figured I'd have on a bus trip, but it felt good. I'd been a doer this time. I think Scout would be proud.

I smile and read the familiar words, knowing I won't finish the page. Twenty-five hours without sleep and the drone of a moving bus. I'm out till Alabama.

Chapter Eleven

Somewhere in Missouri
March 14, 1986, 10:45 a.m.

In a 1961 interview of Harper Lee
she said she wrote one page a day for her second
book.
If she's still working on it,
I figure she must have almost 10,000 pages by now.

I open my eyes. My head is resting on a shoulder. It's a massive shoulder of green plaid flannel, and worse yet, there's a wet spot where I drooled.

I sit up and wipe my mouth. A guy next to me is drawing in a sketchpad, so absorbed he either doesn't notice me or is being kind.

He turns and nods as if he's been patiently waiting for me to get off his shoulder. His oversized face is framed by long red sideburns that match his unruly red hair. Wire-rimmed glasses frame a slanted nose.

He runs his finger through a red walrus mustache that reaches down to the corners of his mouth. I'm staring into his large eyes, or maybe it's just the glasses that make them seem so big. His look is penetrating, and I feel like an idiot.

"You were pretty zonked. You slept through Columbia and Kingdom City."

"Sorry I used you as a pillow," I apologize.

"Glad to oblige." He hands me my book from his lap. "This fell off while you were sleeping."

"Thanks." I take *Mockingbird* and tuck it in close. "I don't remember you sitting here when I got on."

He smiles. "I wasn't. I boarded at Columbia. There weren't any empty seats. You didn't seem to mind me sitting here. At least, you didn't say anything at the time." He laughs at his own joke and a high-pitched wheezing sound emerges from his throat. The man in front of us turns around and stares as if an alien has just landed on our bus. My seatmate stops laughing and looks down at the floor.

I smile at his odd laugh. I feel embarrassed for him. I know what it's like to be made fun of, but not because of my looks or my laugh. Amy says I'm pretty. I think I'm plain looking, except for the dimple in my right cheek when I smile.

Loud conversations and the whine of fussy children begin to fill my ears. "What time is it?" I shout above the noise. I suddenly remember my dad. I wish I had called him from Kansas City. The air on the bus is warm and heavy, as if crammed with too many bodies. I shake my head, pushing out the sluggishness.

He looks at his watch, which isn't covered by his shirtsleeves because they're three inches too short. In fact, his whole shirt seems too small for his large body.

"It's eleven."

"Oh," I respond, unable to hide the panic in my voice. By now Dad has definitely found my note. Maybe even called the police. I shudder as I think of the trouble I'm in.

"Are you okay?"

I nod. "I just need to make a phone call."

He stares cautiously at the seat in front of him. "St. Louis is an hour from here. We have a layover, so you can get off and use the phone."

"Great." I'm still groggy from four hours of sleep when I'm used to ten. My mouth feels like a sewer, and I haven't brushed my hair since yesterday morning. I open my backpack and rummage through the front pocket in search of gum. I take out two pieces.

"Would you like a stick of gum?"

His eyes widen. "Sure, thanks." He takes the gum, quickly unwraps it, and shoves it into his mouth. "I'm starved. I didn't eat breakfast this morning because I had to be at the bus depot so early." He relaxes back into the seat, his anxiety forgotten. His body melts into the upholstery, reminding me of a softened marshmallow squished between two graham crackers.

"I'm hungry, too." My stomach makes several rumbling noises to back my sudden insight.

The guy looks to be in his mid-twenties, although he might be older. His thick eyebrows arch at the mention of food, and his voice becomes animated.

"When I got on I asked the driver if there's any fast food near the next stop. As you can tell from looking at me, food is my first priority. He said there's a pizza place just down the street from the depot."

"Pizza sounds good." I glimpse at a drawing in his sketchpad.

"Where are you traveling to?"

He sits up tall and speaks with no hesitation. "Across the U.S. I'm taking thirty days to see it all."

I force a nod. "That sounds great. Where are you going first?"

"I think I'll get off in Tennessee somewhere, maybe Memphis. I've never seen the Grand Ole Opry."

"That's in Nashville," I reply, remembering that fact from a movie I saw about Loretta Lynn. "But you can visit Elvis's mansion in Memphis."

"Hey. That's better yet," he drawls in a bad Elvis voice. "I've got the sideburns for it. Maybe I'll dye my hair black and become one of those Elvis impersonators."

I laugh at the thought.

"This is the first time I've taken a Greyhound," he confides. "We never went anywhere while I was growing up, so I decided it was time to see the country. Of course, I'm losing some pay while I'm doing it."

"What do you do?" The bus hits a bump, sending us both into the air for half a second.

"I unload trucks. Exciting work, right? Epp Gobarth's the name." He sticks out his hand and I reach over and give it a squeeze.

"Hi, Epp. I'm Sco—I'm Erin," I correct myself.

"That's okay. Sometimes I forget who I am, too," he says. Then he winks and adds, "Not really."

78

"I guess it's from reading this book so much," I say with a nervous laugh.

He nods. "I read that back in high school. Did you know that's the only book the author ever wrote? She won a big prize for it, too. I think she's dead now."

I smile politely and don't correct him.

He picks up his sketchpad and looks at it. It's a drawing of a cartoon character in some kind of maze. The character is short, with wild frizzy hair much like Epp's hair, and he has round eyes that take up most of his face.

"This is my life's work."

"Are you an illustrator?"

His chubby cheeks bounce with the jiggle of the bus as he shakes his head. "No way. I've been working on a computer game for the last three years, kind of like Zork, you know, a role-playing game but with more action and better graphics. I've been learning computer code in my spare time, and designing this booklet for the game. Only problem is, I was developing it for the Atari 800 personal computer and that's been discontinued."

"When do you think you'll be finished with your game?" I ask, wondering what the point would be now.

He looks down as if he's calculating a mathematical problem. "Don't know. I'll have to modify the code for a new system. I keep adding things. This maze is my latest addition."

I look it over. The complex maze has over thirty paths that stretch down and around the paper. I follow one path with my eyes and end up next to a grenade. "I like it. You have a good eye for detail." Epp brightens at my remark.

"This sketch is not as complex as the graphics will be. I'm continually upgrading it. Of course the new system will need 128K of memory to play."

He's lost me but I try to pay attention and end up focusing on his red eyebrows, which twitch as he speaks. It's almost hypnotic, and I'd love to go back to sleep, but Epp isn't about to stop his private lesson on the design of his computer game. I nod as he talks, and I figure the half hour that follows makes up for at least one day of missed school.

Chapter Twelve

Like the Rubik's Cube that I've never been able to master,
things just don't line up right for me.
Why didn't Dad remarry when I was two years old?
I would have called her Mommy.
She could have taught me how to make chocolate chip cookies and crochet.
And I could have acted embarrassed when she showed up at school
with the lunch I left at home.
All those "mom" things that I envy about Amy and her mother.
I'm too old to have a mom now.
Susan doesn't act like she wants the job anyway.
She just wants to be my friend.

"What a dumb thing to do, Erin!" My brother's sarcastic voice reaches out over the miles and hits me right in the chest. "Dad freaked out. He even called the cops."

I groan, the weight of guilt settling in as I imagine my face plastered on a milk carton in Baltimore.

"Why did he call?" I can't finish because Dad is yelling at Jeff to give him the phone.

A muffled sound interrupts the yells, then I hear Dad's echoing voice. "Erin, are you all right?"

"I'm fine," I insist. I steel myself for the onslaught.

"My God, we've been worried sick," his voice cracks, and I swallow hard. "Tell me where you are and we'll come get you."

I was ready for screaming and shouting, but not this.

I almost cave. Maybe I should let him wire me some money and take the bus back home. Or I could hang out here till Dad drives down to pick me up. But then I think of Sedushia's encouraging words when we parted. I think of how far I've already come. I can't go home. Not like this.

"I'm sorry I didn't call sooner, Dad. I didn't mean to worry you."

"Is this about Susan and me? Never mind, we'll talk about it when I get there. Just tell me where you are."

I cover the receiver with my hand as a voice from an overhead speaker blares out that a bus to Kansas City departs in ten minutes.

"There's something I have to do, Dad. I'm not ready to come home yet."

An uncomfortable silence follows. "Does this have to do with your mother's diary?"

"Why didn't you tell me Mom used to write?" I blurt it out in accusation.

"Listen, Erin, we'll talk about it on the way back. Where are you?" His voice is higher, to the point of exasperation.

A long pause follows. I want to say the right thing. I don't want to make him mad, but somehow that seems hopeless now. How can I explain to him what I'm doing when I don't even know myself? How can I describe the drive I feel inside to do this? I can't. I don't want to break down and cry on the phone, so I do the only thing I can think of that will keep me on this trip.

I hang up.

I close my eyes and force back the tears. Now I'm really in trouble.

I turn around and run into Epp, who is coming out of the men's restroom. He's wearing a pouch that fastens around the middle, but it sits below his protruding stomach and can barely be seen.

"Sorry," Epp apologizes, even though it's clearly my fault.

"Let's get some lunch," he suggests when he looks at my face. I quickly rub my eyes and nod.

I end up standing in line behind him at a busy fast-food pizza restaurant. Epp asks if I want to split a large pizza, but I'm low on cash. I order one slice and a Coke. Fifteen minutes later, I manage to grab a small corner table where I wash down my cheese pizza while Epp sits across from me finishing off a large combo.

"Where's the beef?" He says when he sees my pizza, then laughs. Two women from a nearby table overhear him and laugh as well.

"I can live on this stuff," Epp says between stuffing his face with large bites. "I usually eat cold pizza for breakfast."

I frown. "I don't know if I could stomach cold pizza in the morning."

"Food is food. I've even eaten ice cream for breakfast when I was out of groceries," he says.

The pizza place is bustling with the lunch crowd, mostly people from our bus. A tall, dark-haired man stands in line and reminds me of my father. Dad's good looks turn even my friends' heads. Amy said it's a miracle he didn't remarry years ago.

"I could handle ice cream for breakfast," I reply. "Of course, my dad would have a fit if I did."

Epp nods. "Yeah. When I lived at home, my mom got on me about my eating habits. She said she didn't want to see me die young of heart disease like my dad. I have the same build as he did *and* the same appetite."

Epp sounds like a poster boy for future heart problems. "Doesn't all that worry you?"

He shrugs and wipes pizza sauce from the corner of his mouth, smearing it onto his cheek. He doesn't notice the two drops of pizza sauce on the front of his shirt. "I don't think about it much. I'm not as bad as my dad was. He smoked and drank. I don't do either of those things."

"My mom died a week after I was born. It was some freak thing. She hemorrhaged and didn't go to the doctor soon enough." I stop and put my hand over

85

my mouth. I already spilled my guts to Sedushia, and now I'm telling another stranger about my mom.

Epp pauses between bites. "That's gotta be tough on you. No memories. At least I had my dad around while I was growing up. We both loved football and never missed a Rams home game."

"I wish I'd known my mom." I unzip my backpack and take out Mom's diary, opening it to the page about Harper Lee. "My mom wrote this back in 1963. I love to write and didn't know I had anything in common with her until now."

Epp takes the diary and reads the excerpt about Mom's desire to be a writer and her letter to Harper Lee. His large eyes grow even bigger.

"Wow," he says when he finishes. "Did Harper Lee write back to her?"

"I don't know. I didn't find a letter."

"If she did, I'll bet it's valuable now."

I shrug. I hadn't thought of any value except a personal one.

"So you're a writer?"

"I like to write," I clarify. "And I'm a huge Harper Lee fan."

"Right," he says as if it's suddenly clear. I look down at my backpack. I'm afraid I've told him too much. I don't know why I felt compelled to share Mom's diary entry with him. Maybe it's because he shared his sketches with me.

"Did your mother ever publish a book?"

"There are a few stories toward the end of her diary. All I know is that she quit college when she was nineteen to marry my dad." I push leftover pizza crust around on my plate. "I think she ran out of time."

Epp rests his chin in one hand in a thoughtful pose. "Maybe she didn't want to have a book published. Maybe she just wanted to write for herself."

"Most people write to be published," I reply, thinking of Epp's game that nobody will ever see.

Epp hands me the diary. A smudge of pizza sauce dots the edge where his finger touched the page, but he doesn't seem to notice. I wipe the smudge with my napkin, and Epp's face turns red.

"Sorry. I should have been more careful."

I shake my head like it's nothing. "It's okay." I put her diary in my backpack as I talk. "I know my mom wanted to be a writer when she wrote to Harper Lee."

"I guess you're right. She must have had some big goals to send a letter to a famous writer. It'd be like me writing to Joel Berez."

"Who?"

"He's the CEO of Infocom. Of course, I would never send my game idea to him."

"Why not?"

He picks up a piece of pizza and pauses with it hanging in midair. "What if Harper Lee told your mom to forget about writing? To be honest, I couldn't take the criticism. It might sound stupid, but this game has become a dream of mine. Without it, I'm just some nerd who lives alone, works at a boring job, plays computer games, and watches too many James Bond movies. But this game"——he nods toward a man behind the counter stretching pizza dough onto a pan ——"it makes me a work in progress, like that pizza."

It figures he would use food as a comparison. Now I know why I showed him Mom's diary. I'm like Epp. We both have far-fetched dreams. Maybe that's why I write. Maybe that's why I'm obsessive about *Mockingbird.* Those things make me feel special, like there's hope for me, too.

One thing I like about Scout's story is that it's told from a child's point of view, but also from the distance of an adult looking back on her childhood. And sometimes she sort of wavers between the two, like she's not sure which one belongs, like she's caught in the middle.

Chapter Thirteen

Interstate 55 South
March 14, 1986, 3:00 p.m.

I'm reading each entry slowly,
absorbing every word.
Mom didn't filter her thoughts
like I do in my journal,
searching for a finished product
that will sound better than I really am.

Epp has been quiet since we left St. Louis. I'm wondering if it has something to do with what happened when I stopped to buy gum. Epp was fishing through his pockets for change because he wanted a candy bar from the vending machine. Two kids approached him. They were wearing matching Celtics shirts with the number 32 plastered on the front. Kevin McHale's number, one of many pieces of sports trivia I've picked up from home. The boys looked to be about eight or nine, which immediately made me suspicious. I've done a lot of babysitting, and that's the worst age for kids. I'd rather have five babies than one nine-year-old. The two kids were both grinning like they were up to something.

"Hey, mister, is that your girlfriend?" one of them asked, pointing at me.

"She's a girl and she's a friend, but no, she's not my girlfriend," Epp replied with more patience than I would have shown.

"That's because you're a gargantuan freak," the other boy yelled, as the first one kicked Epp in the shin, causing him to drop all the coins in his hand. The brat then ran away, yelling "The freak has a girlfriend" at the top of his lungs.

Epp shook his head and I looked down at the fallen change.

"You should have belted them," I told him after I'd chased a runaway quarter under a cracked plastic chair that was bolted onto the dirty tiled floor. The candy machines were tucked away in a corner next to a row of old metal lockers, many of them missing doors, and no one noticed the commotion, not even a scruffy man sprawled out on the floor near the soda machine.

"They're just kids," Epp said. "Besides, I've been called a lot worse."

It didn't help matters when the two boys got on the same bus as we did. I would have yelled at their parents or complained to the bus driver, but Epp didn't say a word, even when the boys snickered and pointed at him. A born gentleman, he helped two elderly women up the stairs of the bus, taking one by the elbow, then hopping back down to assist the other. They both smiled gratefully, then sat as far away from us as possible.

Epp is now leaning back in his seat, one knee propped up, doodling on his sketchpad, seemingly unfazed by the incident that I'm still fuming over. He's much more forgiving than I am. The boy asked if I was Epp's girlfriend. Only a jerky kid would think a twenty-something guy would date a sixteen-year-old. Plus Epp isn't exactly boyfriend material. First, he's too old. I know only one girl in my class who dated a guy that age, and she's got a bad reputation. Then there's the fact that he's a nerd, although a nice one.

Everything annoys me at this point. Maybe it's the fact that this bus ride seems to go on endlessly from one dirty station with buzzing fluorescent lighting to the next, or maybe I'm just getting crabby. But the drone of the engine is preventing any possibility of sleep.

I'm trying to gather my thoughts for my journal when Epp leans over. "May I?" he asks as his pencil looms above my paper.

"Sure." I hand him my journal so he doesn't have to write sideways.

He begins drawing, and I'm amazed at how easy he makes it look. He sketches a girl, and I soon realize from the ponytail and pug nose that he's drawing me. He draws two moon-shaped eyes that take up much of the face, which seems to be a signature characteristic of his drawings. I've never considered my eyes my best feature, but I keep quiet.

He draws a book in my lap, and scribbles the initials TKAM. Then he pencils in the background, a bus filled with passengers, but the ones in the picture are odd-shaped and all have moon eyes. On the side of the picture he writes *"From Epp Gobarth."*

"Thanks." I hold up the sketch to admire it, then carefully close the journal so as not to smudge the pencil drawing.

"Is your journal like your mom's diary?" he asks.

"Not exactly. My mom wrote in a casual style, except for her stories, which are more thought out. Before this trip I put only my best writing in my journal. But now I'm putting a bit of everything; a few descriptions, poems, whatever I feel at the moment. I like reading those parts the most in Mom's diary."

"How long have you had her diary?"

A sudden itch in my throat makes me cough. "Dad just gave it to me yesterday."

Epp folds his arms. "Are you in trouble?"

"Trouble?" My voice jumps an octave.

"That call you made, was it collect?"

My face reddens. "Yes."

"You know when you make a collect call, it's easy to trace where it came from."

He's right. I am in trouble. I have the worst poker face in the world and Epp is watching me closely. I think he knows.

"I sort of ran away. You're not going to turn me in, are you?"

Epp looks around, as if he's sizing up the rest of the passengers. He leans over and says in a low voice, "I'd feel responsible if anything happened to you. There are a lot of weirdos out there."

I stare at him, wondering if he has any idea what he just said. Most of the other people on the bus think *he's* the weirdo.

His brows furrow. "Why are you running away?"

I look down. "I just wanted to do something my mom never had the chance to do."

"Where are you going?"

"Monroeville, Alabama."

He nods. "How come you're traveling alone? Girls should always travel in groups of two, at least that's what my mom says."

I shrug. It didn't occur to me to ask Amy to come.

"Aren't you afraid to travel by yourself?"

I'd felt safe with Sedushia. Now that she's gone I've been more uncomfortable, even a little scared. But admitting that seems like admitting defeat. "I've done it lots of times," I say sheepishly.

He looks down at his drawing. "Maybe I should come with you."

I want to pretend I didn't hear him, but he sneaks a peek at me. He's holding his breath, as if it took all his courage to say that.

"What about Memphis?" I remind him.

He waves his hands in the air and I sink down in my seat. "I have thirty days. I can go anywhere I want."

I don't really mind him coming. I like the thought of someone sitting next to me now, if just for the conversation. But I can't fathom why he'd want to ride fifteen hours on the bus when Memphis is only a few hours away. "We just met this morning. Why would you do that?"

He pauses, as if he's searching for words. "I think that maybe you should go home. But I'm not a snitch, and I couldn't face the rest of my trip knowing I left a kid alone and wondering what happened to her. So as a compromise, I'll ride the bus with you to make sure you get to . . . where are you going again?"

"Monroeville, Alabama," I repeat.

His eyes light up. "Great. I've never been there. What's in Monroeville?"

I look down at my journal and whisper, "Harper Lee."

Chapter Fourteen

Cape Girardeau, Missouri
March 14, 1986, 4:10 p.m.

Everything makes me think of Dad:
a man carrying his daughter on his shoulders,
the announcer's voice blaring from a boom box
behind us.
Dad bought me my first bra,
a training bra that he picked out himself.
Dad deserves better than me.

Epp is eating a Hershey bar while leaning over his
Rand McNally atlas, trying to find the small dot that
represents Monroeville. Bits of chocolate flutter on the
pages, and he flicks them off with the side of his hand.

"In twelve more hours, we'll be in Montgomery,
Alabama. That's just a couple of hours north of
Monroeville," he announces.

It's after four o'clock in the afternoon. My rear end is sore from eighteen-plus hours of sitting. The engine sounds have caused a permanent humming in my ears. I've had to go to the bathroom since Perryville, but Sedushia warned me never to use the bathroom on the bus. My legs are crossed, as if holding back a potential flood. I stand up. The small cubicle at the back of the bus has the IN USE sign in place and a woman waiting outside. I'll have to hold it till we make it to Sikeston.

"If I'd had more money, I could have flown to Alabama. It's a four-hour flight from Minnesota."

Epp shakes his head. "You meet more interesting people on the bus."

A woman wearing a heavy parka holds a covered basket on her lap. Two rows back from her a man talks to himself as he clutches a brown paper bag. I wonder what's in that bag. The two Jesse James boys run up and down the aisle when the driver's not yelling at them.

Then there's the baby that's been crying since Jackson, Missouri. The bald man in front of me leaned his seat back as far as it can go and is snoring loudly, with long stretches between each snort that make me wonder if he's going to stop breathing. I've even bumped his seat when the pauses go beyond twenty seconds, which is the longest time I've counted so far.

Epp's shirt has developed an odor, with bits of food thrown in to boot. The entire bus smells bad, but I can't pinpoint any single smell, just a barrage of stinks hitting me at any given moment. I think it's worse in the back by the bathroom.

Epp stares out the window, as if he's memorizing every bit of landscape on his journey. "So you say Harper Lee is still alive. Why do you suppose she never wrote another book?"

"She may have written more books. She just never published another one."

"Why not?"

I have several theories on this. Most of them are pretty far-fetched. "You said that not everyone writes for publication. I'm sure she has her reasons."

Epp scrunches up his mouth and his walrus mustache creases. "You think *Mockingbird* was too hard to top?"

I pause a moment before answering. "No. Harper Lee is a writer, so that's what she does. Maybe she's just taking her time on her next book."

Epp looks at me. "Why do you think your mom gave up writing?"

I shake my head. "I don't know. It's odd, but when I asked my dad, he sounded like he didn't want to talk about it."

Neither of us speaks for a minute, then Epp turns to face me.

"It's not his fault. You can't blame him for that."

"For what?"

"For her quitting. Just because they married. Maybe your mom intended to go back to writing after you were older. My mom didn't work until my dad died. Now she's a full-time clerk at Penney's."

"It's not just that. He didn't seem to know she wanted to be a writer. You're supposed to know everything about the person you marry. This was a big part of her life, at least it was at sixteen."

Epp breaks open a bag of Cheez Doodles and lets out a sigh. "People change."

I want to tell him that I love to write. But I'm afraid I don't have what it takes. If my mom quit, what's to say I won't? Harper Lee gave up law school to write her novel. Mom gave up writing to have a family. What will I have to give up?

"I won't change," I announce to Epp.

He frowns as though he doesn't believe me. "Change isn't necessarily bad. Besides, how are you going to prevent it?"

"I could quit school and become a writer now." As soon as I say it I realize how stupid an idea it is.

"Are you crazy? You can't quit school. I should know. If I'd gone to college, I'd be programming computers instead of unloading trucks and learning computer code in my spare time."

I brush off a piece of chocolate that made its way onto the armrest. "What about writers who escape from life, who run off to secluded spots to write?"

He cocks his head and looks smug. "How many of them never finished high school, let alone college? Did Harper Lee graduate from college?"

"Yup. She even went to law school, then dropped out one year shy of getting her law degree."

Epp points his finger at me like a loaded gun. "Then I'd say you have a few years to go."

What does he know about it? I turn away from him. "I can make that decision myself, thank you."

He takes out his sketchpad and starts drawing. "Fine by me. I'm just along for the ride."

Now it seems like he's along to ruin my ride. Just because I'm young doesn't mean I can't make my own decisions.

I hope Harper Lee will see it my way. She once wrote an article about discovering America and how her fifteen-year-old nephew hitchhiked across the country. He didn't need some big oaf wearing a pizza-stained flannel shirt tagging along either.

I open my journal and wait for our next stop, but it's hard to concentrate. Epp Gobarth is way too exasperating. He's an obsessive eater, and I'm sitting on cracker crumbs and chocolate candy that he spilled on my seat. He acts like he wants to help, but I know what he's really trying to do. He's trying to talk me into going home. Of course it isn't going to work, and him tagging along isn't going to stop me either. One thing I know for certain though. If he stays on the bus, I'm switching seats in Sikeston.

Chapter Fifteen

Near Hayti, Missouri
March 14, 1986, 6:05 p.m.

Scout is a funny kid who reminds me of myself.
She's not very fond of school.
At times she's a trial to her father,
and she understands how peculiar people can be.
That's why I love Mockingbird.
I wonder if that's why my mom loved it, too.

I follow Epp back on to the bus after a twenty-five-minute stop, most of which I spent trying to avoid him. He plops down in the window seat, and I keep walking. An elderly woman sits near the back reading *People* magazine. Using my most respectful voice, I ask if I can sit next to her. She smiles sweetly.

"Of course, dear."

Epp watches from his seat. I quickly look away and sit down.

"Weren't you sitting with your brother before?" the woman asks.

"Oh, he's not my brother."

"Really?" Her voice drips with suggestion. My face reddens. "He's, um, my cousin," I stammer, but I don't think she buys it.

"Hmm," she says as she pinches her mouth tight and turns away from me.

I'm not one to stay where I'm not wanted, so I stand and walk up the aisle, then sit down next to Epp, who is busy sketching.

He looks over at me. "You're mad at me, aren't you?"

I shrug and open my book.

Epp rubs his face. "I always mess things up. Do you want me to get off the bus? Because I will if I'm bothering you."

"No." My voice is almost a shout. "No," I say again softer, since people are looking at us.

Epp shifts in his seat. "I thought I should talk you into staying in school," he says. "But that's not my call."

My book is perched open in front of me, even though I'm not really reading the words. I'm thinking about Dad, and Jeff, who will tell everyone at school what I did and what an idiot I am. Why am I on this bus? What am I trying to accomplish besides being grounded for the next six months?

Epp leans over. "I'm really sorry."

"You know," I say, closing my book and putting it down. "I've been having second thoughts. What's the point in causing my dad so much grief? Maybe I should go home before I get into more trouble."

His eyebrows twitch. "Sounds like you might be giving up."

"I'm tired. We still have such a long way to go."

Maybe it's the exhaustion, but I feel as though I could burst into tears. My throat tightens and my chest feels heavy. "On top of everything else, it's my birthday and I'm spending it on a bus."

"It's obvious that this trip is important to you," Epp says, nodding for emphasis. "I hate to admit it, but I would never have had the courage to do what you're doing."

He doesn't get it. "My dad called the cops. It's just a matter of time before my dad finds me."

Epp clutches his sketchpad. "You're not going to let that stop you, are you? Listen, I didn't mean to take away your spirit." He looks around the bus. "Maybe I can make it up to you." He stands and pushes past me into the aisle. The bus turns sharp, and Epp hangs on to my seat to keep from falling. He takes up a good portion of the aisle, and I wonder if another sudden turn might cause him to fly across the bus and land on the bratty kid who kicked him earlier.

He puts one hand into the air and waves at the passengers, then turns toward the front of the bus and does the same.

"Could I have your attention for a moment?" he yells, and everyone but the nonsleeping baby responds.

What is he doing now? I sink down in my seat.

"I have an announcement to make. Erin is making an extraordinary journey to Monroeville, Alabama." He points at me, and I slide down and cover my face with my hands.

"It's a pilgrimage inspired by something her mother wrote almost twenty-five years ago. Erin is going to visit Harper Lee, the author of the novel *To Kill a Mockingbird,* and talk to her about writing. Right now, Erin is having some second thoughts about her trip, and I ask all of you to offer your support and prayers to her so that she makes it there."

I want to die. I can hear murmurs throughout the

bus, things like "Is he for real?" and "Who is Harper Lee?"

Epp raises his hands again. "That's all. Thank you," he says, then pushes past me and sits down.

I can't even look at him. All I can do is crouch down in my seat and stare at my book.

Epp leans over. "I bet many of them support you on this. You shouldn't give up."

My face burns at the idea of a busload of eyes fixed on the back of my head. I knew Epp was weird, but I didn't expect this. The people on the bus will soon kick us both off.

Epp sits back contentedly. People in front of us are snickering. I can't take it. I sneak a look: the bathroom is open. No matter how bad it is, I'd rather spend the next two hours in there than out here. I grab my journal and stand up, hoping to make a beeline to the back before anyone notices me. I leave Epp without saying a word.

Suddenly, the sound of clapping breaks through the chatter. The noise is coming from the man with a brown paper bag. The clapping sound spreads to the woman with a basket.

The bus driver shouts, "Way to go," and waves

at me. A few other people nod and clap. The rest ignore me, except for two men who stare and smirk. I walk slowly toward the back until the man with the bag pulls on my sleeve to stop me.

"Don't get discouraged. Follow your dreams," he says and winks.

Two seats back, a woman reaches up to shake my hand. "I don't know who Harper Lee is, but give her my best."

I nod, dumbstruck.

The Jesse James boys clap and smile at me. Is this the same bus I boarded in Kansas City?

I go into the restroom and lock the door. The lid is down and I sit in the tiny cubicle trying to ignore the smell as the bus tosses me into the wall. My pen shakes as I stare at the blank page in my journal, wondering what to make of all this.

I'm waiting for reality to set back in, for the normal sounds to return; someone pounding on the bathroom door, the paper bag man talking to himself in nonsensical sentences. Instead, the sound of music filters back. People are singing "Happy Birthday," led by Epp, no doubt.

Their voices are off-key and the luggage beneath

us bangs out an odd accompaniment. I can't help but smile at the thought of a few strangers wishing me well, even encouraging my crazy plan. I steady my pen and start writing as the words flow out of me. *Scout would love this moment.*

Chapter Sixteen

Memphis, Tennessee
March 14, 1986, 8:00 p.m.

Christmas is usually spent skiing.
It's easier on Dad that way.
Last Christmas we stayed home.
Susan fixed a turkey, and Dad
made hot buttered rum.
Later, we all played Yahtzee.
For one day we seemed normal,
like any other family celebrating the holidays.
I'd never seen Dad so happy.
I enjoyed it, too.

"We may have trouble," Epp says as he leans forward in his seat. He watches the approaching depot in downtown Memphis, his eyes glued ahead.

There's a uniformed man waiting by the curb. He

isn't wearing a police uniform, but what looks like guard attire. I have a sick feeling that he's waiting for me.

I let out a heavy sigh. "Well, I made it to Memphis." I open my book, waiting for *Mockingbird* to guide me. It's like Atticus waiting for Tom Robinson's sentence. He knows he gave it his best shot but that it won't change the results. He knows what's going to happen.

Epp stands up and walks to the front. He spends a moment talking to the driver.

The bus pulls up next to the curb, where the guard is waiting. The bus driver steps out and speaks to the guard. Epp comes back and picks up his jacket.

The passengers file off. Several of them wave at me and give me the thumbs-up sign.

"We have a one-hour layover," Epps says. "Let's get off and find something to eat."

The guard is no longer there.

I flash a questioning look at Epp, who ignores me and picks up his sketchpad.

"Come on. You don't want to sit here for the next hour, do you?"

I shake my head and grab my book. We walk several blocks to the corner of Beale and South Main. A nine-foot bronze statue of Elvis looks down at us, a guitar at his side, his hip thrust in typical Elvis style, and his arm outstretched like he's welcoming us to his town.

"Well, I can say I saw Elvis." Epp seems satisfied. "Now let's eat."

The street is bustling with hotels and restaurants. Music floats from open doorways. Epp leads me into a sports restaurant, a sit-down type with TVs blaring in the corners, all of them focused on a basketball game. It's after eight and I haven't eaten since the pizza in St. Louis, except for a few M&M's that Epp shared with me.

Epp asks the waitress for a booth, and we settle in across from each other. A glass of water and a menu is placed in front of me.

A sandwich costs about three dollars. Even though I should be rationing my money, the melting cheese oozing over ham piled high on a sesame roll is too good to resist. I glance at Epp above my menu.

"What did you say to the driver?"

Epp focuses on a passing tray of food. "I asked him where I could find a good restaurant within walking distance."

I roll my eyes. "What else?"

"I told him the truth. That people might be looking for you. I don't know what he said to the guard. I don't even know if the guard was looking for you."

"But what if he was?"

Epp shrugs. "Maybe he told him that you already got off the bus."

"Why would he risk lying for me?"

"I don't know. I guess people are rooting for you, Erin. They want you to make it to Monroeville." He stops and adds, "Myself included."

Epp seems different to me now. He won over a bunch of strangers on the bus with embarrassing honesty. He's not so weird. He's just eccentric, like Sedushia. I wonder if people make that mistake about him all the time.

The waitress comes back.

"Y'all ready to order?"

"I'll take the ham and cheese sandwich with the chips."

Epp clears his throat. "I'll have the Monster Burger with extra cheese, a double order of fries, and a Coke."

"Is there a phone?" I ask, and she directs me to the hallway in front of the bathrooms.

"Are you calling home?" Epps asks.

I nod. "Just to let Dad know I'm okay. But I'm not telling him where I am or where I'm heading."

Epp puts his hands up in defense. "No complaints here."

Noise from the kitchen empties out into the hall-way, and I put a hand over one ear while I dial zero.

"I want to make a person-to-person collect call," I shout at the operator, "to Ken Garven from Erin."

A moment later Jeff's faint voice answers the phone and the operator announces a person-to-person collect call for Ken Garven. "He's not here," Jeff replies.

Not there? I've been gone since last night. Why isn't Dad at home worrying about me?

"That party is not available," the operator tells me.

"Jeff," I yell. But the operator cuts us off before he hears me. I hang up and stare at the wall. Jeff would have accepted the call if he knew it was from me. Should I call back and ask for Jeff? How could Dad leave? Doesn't he want to talk to me? I walk back to our booth.

"What did he say?" Epp asks.

"Nothing," I answer flatly. "He wasn't home."

Epp's eyebrows go up.

"Maybe he's at Susan's," I speculate. "She's his fiancée. He just proposed yesterday. It makes sense that he'd want to be with her." I rip the corner of my napkin. How could he go out when his daughter is missing?

"Is that why you left home?"

I shake my head. "No. That has nothing to do with my leaving." Epp's eyes reflect his disbelief.

"Maybe a little," I confess, "but I guess it's time he remarried, you know, before he's too old. It just seems like once Dad's married I'll never get the chance to talk to him about Mom."

Epp's voice rises and he sounds frustrated. "So instead you leave home? Maybe it's time you found a way to talk to him."

"I know," I say almost apologetically.

We're both quiet for a long moment, listening to the gibberish of voices blended with loud music blaring from the bar. Epp appears lost in thought. "I think this trip has more meaning than you realize," he finally says as though he's convinced of that fact. "But what if Harper Lee won't talk to you?"

My hand involuntarily pats down the cover of *Mockingbird*. I push my finger against a small tear at the lower front corner of the jacket. "I've thought about that. You remember how Atticus lost his case? He said there's honor in trying. There's even honor in defeat."

Epp's face turns white and he grips his sketchpad. I think I just hit a nerve.

Chapter Seventeen

Heading South on U.S. 78
March 14, 1986, 9:00 p.m.

I've been straining my eyes in the darkness.
There's an abandoned church at the side of the
road,
with a partly caved-in roof, and dark windows
without glass,
as if forgotten by time.
The church is surrounded by a sea of crimson
clover,
and it looks at peace.
It seems to be telling me something.
But what is it saying?

I take two bites of my sandwich and pick at the chips, debating whether to call home again. Epp makes up for my lack of appetite. He eats every last bite of his meal, even finishing the chips that I couldn't eat. He dribbles ketchup on his shirt and dabs it off with a napkin, also finally noticing the stains from this afternoon's pizza. Then he leaves a huge tip of three dollars. I reluctantly put three quarters on the table, then pick one up when Epp isn't looking. Afterward, we walk back to the bus, peeking in the windows of fancy hotels that have marble floors, enjoying the night air as we carry our heavy winter coats. Fifty degrees seems like a blast of summer air compared with the weather back home.

Six people got off the bus in Memphis, and five new passengers got on. There seems to be a different mood on the bus now. People are beginning to talk to one another. Several women take turns with the crying baby, who ran out of steam after Memphis. The boy who just hours ago kicked Epp in the shin plays him in a game of rock, paper, scissors.

I write in my journal about the landscape and sights I've seen along the road, the shanties on one side and huge estates with gated pillars on the other, the soil that's changed from the familiar black to a rusty red. The most noticeable change is the green that's everywhere, as if the land awoke somewhere between Minnesota and Mississippi and I missed it.

Amy says that the key to good writing is an incredible opening that grabs your attention, like the topping on a pizza. I think it's the language, which I guess is more like the crust. I asked Epp what he thought, and he said it depends on your taste.

I told Epp about Sedushia. It seems like ages ago that I was in Kansas City. Images of home push their way into my thoughts. Did Dad miss work on account of me? Did Amy miss me at school today? Did she hang a Mickey Mouse balloon on my locker like she always does on my birthday? I'm going to buy a postcard in Montgomery and send it to her. A belated show of friendship is better than nothing.

"Stop," Epp cries in defeat to his new best friend. He rubs his hand, which is red from being hit by too many rocks over scissors. Epp should know that rock would be the kid's favorite pick.

It's after nine o'clock and the landscape has faded into dark, indistinguishable shapes. This has been the longest day of my life. I hope to get in a nap because in a couple of hours we'll be entering Alabama, and by five a.m. we'll be in Montgomery, and I'm sure I won't be able to sleep after that. From Montgomery, we'll catch a smaller bus that will take us to Monroeville, less than two hours south.

"Aren't you getting tired?" I ask the rock, paper, scissors kid, who gives me one of his devilish grins and replies, "Nope."

I want to tell him to get lost, but it might ruin the upbeat mood on the bus. I'm getting closer to Monroeville. I could actually make it there. I should be in better spirits.

I take out Mom's diary and read a few entries again. I search for mention of a letter from Harper Lee, but I can't find one. Instead, I find a funny entry about seeing the Beatles on TV. By the time I finish reading it, my mood has lifted.

"You nervous?" Epp asks, and I almost drop the journal. Jesse James's mother finally called him back to his seat, and Epp has been watching me.

"Sort of," I confess, and Epp nods as if he knew it all along. "I feel like I'm on one of those shows where the camera is following my every move." I turn around suspiciously. "And you don't want to mess up one little bit."

"Nobody is going to know what happens once you get off this bus," Epp says. "It's not like I'm sending out a newsletter or calling the *New York Times*."

I relax into my seat. "Good. Because I don't do well

under pressure. Just ask my Spanish teacher. Vocabulary words disappear from my head the moment she gives a test."

"You'll do fine."

I bite down on my lip for a second. "I know it sounds dumb, but I miss my dad." I pause and add, "And my brothers, sort of."

I turn toward the window. "I guess I should go home after I meet Harper Lee. I don't think I'm cut out for life on the road."

The shine from an overhead light bounces off Epp's glasses. "Good. Because I'm afraid you'd end up as roadkill."

Epp reminds me of Jeff now. I give him a playful punch on the shoulder.

"I would not," I object.

Epp rubs his shoulder. "Seriously speaking, my mom always says that the road is as long as you make it. It can be full of snakes or fields of flowers."

"That's sweet. I never thought of it that way."

"Do you read any other books?" Epp asks as he points at *Mockingbird*.

"Of course. But I just keep coming back to this one. There are so many layers."

"I can't remember, does it have anything to say to a computer nerd who's afraid of failure?"

I hand Epp my book. "Go for it."

Epp looks doubtful and presses the book back into my hands. "I haven't read fiction in years. Maybe later."

"But this book has a guarantee. Anyone who doesn't enjoy it will receive a sensitivity refund."

"You couldn't buy publicity like that," Epp quips. "You're a writer's dream."

"Not every writer," I clarify. "And not every book. Just *Mockingbird*."

Chapter Eighteen

Near Hamilton, Alabama
March 15, 1986, 12:30 a.m.

My mother stands in front of me.
She looks like the picture I have of her on my
nightstand.
Her hair is held back with a clip and
she's holding me to her cheek.
I'm just a few days old.
My eyes are half open,
my tiny brows narrowed down over wrinkled,
new-baby skin.
My mother looks tired but happy.
Suddenly I'm no longer in the picture.
She's standing alone in the room.
She turns and looks at me with piercing blue eyes.
"Did you enjoy your sixteenth birthday?" she
asks faintly.
"What?" I strain to hear her.

"Happy birthday. I almost forgot about this."

I open my eyes at Epp's words. From his jacket pocket, he produces a small cupcake wrapped in plastic, pink frosting smudged into the wrapping like a flattened bug on a bus window.

"I know it's not exactly what you had in mind, but it's all I could come up with at that last restaurant." He hands me the cupcake.

"It's great," I reassure him. "Thanks."

"You're not bummed you spent your birthday on a bus?"

"Heck, no. I spent the entire twenty-four hours with three terrific people: Sedushia, you, and my mom." I clutch her diary in my lap.

"Oh," he says as though he just thought of it, "I have something else for you." Epp stands up and accidentally bangs his head on an overhead luggage rack.

"Ouch," he yells, rubbing at the sore spot. The man in front of us wakes up.

"Sorry about that," Epp says to the man when he turns around.

"That's okay," the man replies with a tired voice.

Epp reaches up and takes a booklet out of a small briefcase. He holds it reverently.

"I know you saw the sketch I was working on. This is the book that goes with the game." He hands it to me. "I'm going to let you be the first."

"The first what?"

"To read about my game. It has all the hints for each level. There are graphs and a few pictures so you can make sense of it all. I also have the computer code with me, but I won't bore you with that."

He brought along computer code? He's asking the wrong person. I still can't make sense of Space Invaders. "I don't play computer games," I explain.

Epp ignores my comment. "I've been thinking about what you said at the restaurant, the lesson you learned from that book about honor in trying, even in failure. You're sharing your trip with me. I want to share my game with you."

I flip through it. Thirty-two pages of small type, diagrams, and pictures. "This is way different, Epp."

"Just the same, your opinion really matters to me."

"Okay," I relent. "But I warn you. I don't know a thing when it comes to this stuff." I take the booklet and glance at Epp's watch. It's past two in the morning.

"Have fun," he says, then excuses himself.

The air feels cooler now. I want to snuggle inside my coat and go back to sleep. Instead, I suppress a yawn, flick on the overhead light, and start reading. How could Epp actually enjoy doing this? The main character is an elf dressed in fatigues and carrying a large weapon. He looks like a cross between a Smurf and G.I. Joe.

The first scene is set in the office of the president of the United States. The goal is to save the president, who has been abducted by terrorists and flown to some unnamed country. Only G.I. Smurf can save him, because he is the best-trained secret agent they have. He is given three things that will come in handy for his mission: a compass, ammunition, and a map of tunnels. Some of the tunnels will provide clues, and they'll all hold danger.

The overhead light isn't bright enough to read the small type. I hold the booklet up, closer to the light.

"Here. Use this." I turn around. A guy with a crew cut who got on in Memphis hands me a flashlight.

"Thanks," I whisper. He asks if he can sit in the seat till Epp returns. He looks about my age.

I have trouble finding the switch for the flashlight, a pocket type on a key chain.

"Here," the guy says as he reaches for the flashlight. "Like this." He turns the top and the light comes on. "I'm Billy. Did that guy really design a game?" His heavy Southern drawl is full of admiration.

"Yeah, he did. Epp wants me to read it, but it's Greek to me."

"I'm into this stuff. Maybe I could help."

I worry that Epp might not like it, but then again I'm about to fall asleep. "You wouldn't mind?"

"Not at all," he says as if I'm doing him the favor instead of the other way around.

We hold the booklet between us and shine the light on the page. The rest of the bus is quiet except for a few yawns and shuffling noises.

"Cool graphics," Billy says with an air of experience. "What's your name?" He flips to the next page.

"I'm Erin." This guy is good. He can talk and read at the same time. He shows an eagerness that I don't feel, making comments while he reads, like "Totally sophisticated" and "That's awesome."

"Erin?" Epp is standing in the aisle. He'd been gone so long I almost forgot about him. He's looking at me as if I just sold top-secret information to the enemy.

Billy reaches out to shake his hand. "Hi, Epp. I'm Billy. This game is extreme."

Epp devours the praise. "You really like it?" he asks excitedly. Billy gives him the thumbs-up, and Epp smiles and sits in Billy's seat behind us.

"Are you finished with this page?" Billy asks me.

"Maybe you can explain it," I suggest.

He turns and looks at me; a slow grin spreads across his face, and warmth flushes up from my neck to my cheeks. He has a cute smile.

Chapter Nineteen

Just Past Birmingham, Alabama
March 15, 1986, 2:45 a.m.

Is my fantasy of meeting Harper Lee any different
from Scout's fantasy of meeting Boo Radley,
of sitting on the porch swing
talking about the weather
like friendly neighbors on a first-name basis?
But why do I expect Harper Lee to know me when
I get there?

The lights of passing towns cast dancing shadows across the ceiling of the bus.

"Where you from?" Billy asks me. He holds the flashlight steady, the beam focused on the page in front of him. For the last ten minutes, he's been studying a graph that calculates the difficulty of each level.

"St. Paul, Minnesota. How about you?"

"I'm from Ripley, Tennessee, about an hour north

of Memphis. It's a small town, although we do have a country club." He looks up and adds, "Not that I belong to it. My daddy ran off when I was eight. Makes it hard on my mom. But she just finished her nursing training so she's doing okay now."

I try to digest the sudden rush of information and can only reply, "Oh. That's good."

"You have a dad?" he asks.

I nod. "Yeah. I don't have a mom. She died when I was little."

Billy shakes his head. "My dad might as well have died. I know one thing, I'll never be like him."

I just nod my head again. He smells clean, a definite improvement over Epp.

"How old are you?" he suddenly asks, as he turns the page to yet another graph.

I'm tempted to say I'm eighteen, but I've learned from this trip that I'm a lousy liar and I don't think I can pass for eighteen anyway.

"Sixteen."

"Really? I thought you were older. I've heard talk on the bus about you."

I take in a sudden breath and open my eyes wide.

Billy doesn't seem to notice. He's still staring at the page. "I'm eighteen. I just finished basic training and spent a few weeks back home. I'm heading to the Navy base down in Florida. So"—he glances away from the booklet to give me a quick appraisal, shining the beam of the flashlight on my face—"is it true about you?"

"Well, what have you heard?" I push away the flashlight.

He aims the flashlight on his own face and speaks in a mysterious voice. "That you're on your way to meet with some author. That you're a writer and she invited you to visit her."

Jeez. This is worse than the rumor mill at school.

"Because I think it's way cool," he continues.

I open my mouth to say something, but nothing comes out.

The man in front of us turns around. "When you reach Monroeville, be sure and stop at Mel's Dairy Dream. It's near where Harper Lee's childhood home once stood. 'Course, I reckon she'll tell you that herself, since you're staying with her."

I nod, amazed he knows that piece of trivia, amazed how the story has grown. Soon I expect to be related to Harper Lee.

I get up to use the restroom. It's late, after three in the morning. Epp is dozing behind us. Part of his mustache has slipped into his mouth, and it floats in and out with each breath. I pat him on the shoulder as I walk past. Most of the people are making an effort to sleep, sprawled out in every possible position; others are talking quietly among themselves. I'm exhausted but past the point of tired, if that makes any sense. I sway between the seats with the uneven motion and don't realize that the bathroom is occupied until I reach the back of the bus.

"Erin," someone whispers. It's a woman I remember from before. She's older and heavyset, with tight brown curls tinged with flecks of gray framing her round face. She motions for me to sit down in the seat next to her.

I sit and she leans over. Her soft, Southern accent has a soothing quality. She talks quietly in the darkness. "I'm Helen. I just wanted to tell you how impressed I am that a girl your age would undertake such an endeavor. I'm a Harper Lee fan myself, and I've always wanted to write a novel. It's a pleasure to meet a writer who is so motivated."

"I'm not really a writer," I explain. "I like to write but I haven't been published."

She puts her hand on mine. "Don't sell yourself short. Do you think Harper Lee was a writer before she published *To Kill a Mockingbird*?"

"Yes, of course, but . . ." I stop as I realize what she means.

"And I hear your mother wrote as well," she continues.

I smile.

"My mother was a schoolteacher. I followed in her footsteps. I've taught second grade for thirty years. That's what I'd like to write about. I've got so many stories in my head from all my years of teaching. I just haven't had the time to put my thoughts on paper yet. I envy you. You're already writing and you're so young. It must be in the genes."

"Thanks so much," I say, my confidence boosted by her kind remarks. I excuse myself because the bathroom is now empty. I spend extra time brushing out my hair, leaving it down on my shoulders instead of pulling it back in a ponytail, wondering if Billy will notice. On the way to my seat, someone taps my arm. I flinch until I see his friendly face. It's a man about my dad's age dressed in a Kentucky sweatshirt, a matching cap, and jeans. He has dark skin and short black hair. He looks like he wants to say something, so I make eye contact.

"I'm George," he says as he tips his cap respectfully. "Epp said you're changing buses in Montgomery. You ever hear of the freedom riders?"

"I don't think so," I admit.

"Well, Montgomery is the most historic bus terminal in the nation. Since you're spending some time down here, you should see the sights."

"I'll try," I say as I find my seat and sit down.

The bus pulls to a stop in a parking lot next to a McDonald's. We're in a small town, the name of which I don't remember. They seem to have all run together at this point. The door opens and the smell of diesel seeps in. Several passengers stretch their arms. A woman across from us looks around in bewilderment as though she's not quite awake.

Epp's seat is empty. He's up at the front of the bus talking to the driver. Billy is reading about level four, studying a picture of huge desert scorpions.

Billy looks up from the page. "Would you like a soda? I've got a couple in my bag." He reaches into his pack and pulls out two.

"Sure, I'd like a pop," I reply, showing off my Minnesota slang. He gives me a funny look and hands me a Coke.

Billy glances back at George. "Do you know everybody on this bus?"

I suppress a smile. "Not yet."

The bus lunges forward. Epp returns and stands in

the aisle next to us. His expression is grim. "Jack told me he got a message that the police are looking for a girl. He's wondering if you're that girl."

"Oh no," the bald man in front of us says in dismay as he whispers the news across the aisle.

"Do you think they'll be waiting at the terminal in Montgomery?" I ask.

Epp sighs. "Don't know."

I look down at my book.

"Is there anything we can do to help you?" Billy asks as he closes the booklet.

Epp shakes his head. "There aren't any stops between here and the terminal. We're less than half an hour away. I'm sorry, Erin. Maybe if you call your dad when the police pick you up, he'll let you continue on."

"No," I mutter. "It won't do any good."

My trip may be over soon. The dread of having Harper Lee turn me away was beginning to weigh heavy on my mind. Maybe it's better that I don't find out.

I pick up *Mockingbird* and stare at the cover, searching for an answer. Nothing comes to me but a hollow feeling.

Chapter Twenty

Ever since Dad started dating Susan,
he says I've had an "attitude problem."
I blame Susan.
She didn't fuss over me like Dad's other
girlfriends.
Instead, she gave me a new journal.
Why did Susan have to be so nice?

Half the people on the bus have offered me their condolences. They really thought I'd make it to Monroeville and meet with Harper Lee.

I want to bury my head in the seat in front of me. It was a fly-by-the-seat-of-your-pants plan, and I'm embarrassed at the thought of being picked up by the police in front of all these people.

Actually, it's amazing I made it this far. I know it's because of Epp and Sedushia. I should be grateful.

Billy offers to create a diversion for the police so I can get away.

"Thanks, but I don't want you to get in trouble. You might get arrested and not make it back to the base on time."

"It'd be worth it," he says, and I want to hug him.

Epp has been talking to some of the other passengers. It's just before five o'clock in the morning, but there's so much commotion on the bus you'd think it was the middle of the day. Some people look around in confused silence at the gathering crowd and angrily huddle under their coats, their red eyes casting irritated glances my way. But there's genuine concern etched in the faces of those around me.

I close my eyes and imagine myself in front of the courthouse in Monroeville, posing with my arm around Harper Lee while a friendly passerby takes our picture. I've heard that if you can visualize an event, you can make it happen. I've tried it before. Of course, it hasn't worked.

A small circle of people has gathered around my seat.

"We have to do something," George says. "Can't let her give up on her dream yet."

"We can't take on the police," Helen objects.

"She's a minor." The man in front points at me. "We could get arrested."

Finally, they decide to talk to the bus driver, Jack.

"We need his support on this," Epp adds.

"Epp, don't," I say.

Epp leans over. "We'll handle it." He marches off to the front with four others.

I hold my breath for what seems like forever. What are they going to do?

Jack picks up the microphone to make an announcement.

"Folks, I know this is off-schedule, but we're making a quick stop at a restaurant just a block from the depot so that one passenger can depart. I ask all of you to remain on the bus until we reach the terminal." He pauses. "Except for Erin."

The whole bus breaks into applause; even those who seem annoyed with me clap. I feel tears start to well up and I try to hide them.

Epp sits next to me.

"Aren't they great?" he says, shaking his head, his voice more raspy than ever.

"They are." I let out a breath. "And so are you."

A few minutes later the bus pulls up to Pancake Heaven.

"Wait for me at the restaurant," Epp says. "I'll check out the situation at the terminal, and see if it's safe to get on the connecting bus."

I stop at the door and turn to the driver. "Thank you so much." Words don't seem enough right now.

"Good luck," he yells, and everyone on the bus waves good-bye. I wave back and see Billy smiling from the window.

I hurry into the restaurant. It's not busy, but several people are nursing coffee mugs and a few are eating an early breakfast. I ask for a booth. The hostess shows me to a red booth hugging a white tabletop, away from the window. She hands me a giant menu, and I hold it up in front of my face in an attempt to stay low until Epp arrives.

I take out my ticket. I'm supposed to transfer to a smaller bus for Monroeville. It doesn't say what time the bus leaves. I wonder if there's a later bus, in case we miss it, and how we're going to get on if the police are looking for me. Do they have a picture of me or just a general description?

A waitress with bright red hair and a bright smile to match approaches. "Y'all need a while to decide?"

"Could I just get a glass of water for now?" I ask.

"Sure thing," she answers with more zest than anybody has the right to have at five in the morning.

Two policemen enter and I feel the panic flare up inside me. I quickly put the menu in front of my face and peek over the top. The waitress seats them across from me and they order coffee.

A glimmer of hope springs up. Maybe they're not looking for me after all.

The hope turns to dismay when two more police enter.

The waitress seats them in another booth and brings me my glass of water on the same tray as the two coffees.

"Thanks," I say, the menu still covering my face.

After twenty minutes Epp still hasn't come and the pressure is getting to me. I haven't ordered yet, so I just put a quarter on the table and grab my bag. The waitress is bringing out more cups of coffee. I stand and hurry past her.

"I just remembered something. Have to run," I say. She opens her mouth, but I'm already out the door.

The station is half a block down and I start to walk, tugging at the backpack pinching my shoulders, wishing I'd packed lighter. I have a bad feeling. I want to know what's going on but I don't want to go inside. A group of smokers huddle near the door; the red tips of the cigarettes glow in the early-morning light.

I approach the building at a slow pace.

"Hurry, Epp," I whisper. Maybe he had to use the restroom and that's what's taking so long. Or else the police are questioning him. I don't want anyone to get into trouble on my account.

I spot a security guard standing just inside the building. I turn around and head back the other way.

There's a shout behind me. "Hey, you. Stop."

I pick up my pace and make it partway down the street before I'm caught.

Chapter Twenty-one

The Bus Depot in Montgomery, Alabama
March 15, 1986, 5:30 a.m.

I glance innocently up at the guard, but he returns my look with a glare.

"What's your name, girl?" he demands in a heavy accent filled with anger. I can tell he's not going to give me any breaks.

I stare at him, too scared to speak.

"Well? I asked you your name!" His voice thunders down the street, and the smokers turn to watch us.

"There you are." Epp's breathy voice rises behind me. He's pulling a large green suitcase on rollers and running as fast as he's able.

"This is my little sister," he says, and I hold my breath. I don't look anything like Epp.

The guard stares at Epp for a long time. "We're looking for a runaway about her age." He turns to me. "Next time," he scolds, "don't run."

"Sorry," I say, like it was no big deal, just a misunderstanding. He turns and leaves, and we hurry back toward the restaurant, where four more officers await us inside. We don't talk until we're almost in front of Pancake Heaven.

I grab Epp's arm. "You came just in time. He was ready to cuff me."

Epp has to lean over to catch his breath. He hisses out between gasps, "There's an officer by the bus who's looking for you. We can't go back there."

My hands are shaking, flailing about in front of me. "We can't go in the restaurant either. I saw cops in there. How will we get on the bus? What are we going to do?"

Worry is etched on Epp's face. He's probably regretting sitting next to me in the first place, of letting himself get drawn into my stupid dream, kind of like how I felt at Boomer's house. It's bad enough that I've ruined Epp's vacation, but he could also get into trouble helping me. I decide I've caused enough grief.

"This is the end of the line, Epp," I say with more melodrama than I'd planned. "I'm just going to turn myself in."

Epp is silent and I wonder if he agrees with me. I

wish he'd at least try to talk me out of it. Maybe he does want to get rid of me.

Finally he speaks. "Under normal circumstances I would never consider doing this. It isn't a safe way to travel."

"Do what?"

Epp points to two semis in the parking lot of the restaurant. "Hitchhike. We can wait until the drivers of those trucks come out and then ask if they're heading south. Maybe they'll give us a ride."

"What if they won't?"

Epp shrugs. "Let's wait by the furniture truck. That way we'll be out of sight."

We find a spot between the smaller, furniture-delivery truck and a semitrailer. Epp sits on his suitcase. The hard vinyl bows under his weight. I take off my pack and set it on the ground beside me.

We're about one hundred miles from Monroeville. So close compared with how far I've already traveled, over eleven hundred miles in the last thirty-three hours.

"You have to do something for me when we get to Monroeville," Epp says with authority.

I look at him questioningly.

"You have to call your dad and have him come to get you."

"I called him in Memphis," I say in my defense.

"But you didn't talk to him. I don't want to leave you until your dad comes."

I don't want Epp to leave me at this point either.

"Okay." I relent. "I'll call him again. But not until I meet Harper Lee."

Epp considers a moment. "It's a deal."

I feel safe with Epp. The people on the bus who treated him like an outcast are wrong. He's not weird. He's a friend.

Chapter Twenty-two

Parking Lot of Pancake Heaven
March 15, 1986, 6:00 a.m.

Epp reaches out his hand to the driver of the rig. "You wouldn't happen to be heading south, would you?"

The man gives us a guarded look, then nods but doesn't offer his hand in return. "I'm not supposed to pick up hitchhikers. It's against company policy."

My head drops. The man climbs up into his rig and turns the engine over. The noise scares us enough to move a good distance away.

"We can wait for the other driver," Epp suggests, but I have my doubts.

Epp stares at the restaurant as if he's trying to come to a decision. "I'm going to run and use the restroom," he finally says.

"Right now?" My voice raises an octave.

"I'll hurry," he insists. He leaves his luggage and

jogs into Pancake Heaven. What can you say when nature calls?

I sit down in the middle of the bags. We can't wait here all day and ask every person for a ride. Sooner or later the police will come out of the restaurant. What will happen then?

I jump at the sound of an engine turning over. The driver of the other truck came out and I didn't even see him. He's going to leave without us. I climb up the side and knock on the driver's window.

"Stop!" I yell.

The truck's engine rattles and shuts down. I hop off and watch as a man leaps down from the cab.

"I almost didn't see you." He's wagging a finger at me.

"Sorry. I need a ride south," I say softly.

"But I'm not supposed to . . ." He stops and stares at me. "A pretty girl like yourself traveling all alone? Maybe I could make an exception."

I suddenly wish I hadn't knocked on his window.

Epp returns at that moment. "Are you all right, sis?" he asks.

"Oh, yeah," I insist. "He's giving us a ride."

"Great," Epp says as he extends his hand to the

man. The driver looks at Epp and laughs nervously before shaking.

Then the man turns and eyes me suspiciously. "You got a good racket going. I'm only traveling as far as Pensacola. Where you heading?"

"Monroeville."

He nods. "I can do that."

Epp helps me up into the cab. It's kind of a tight squeeze with the three of us. I sit in the middle, balancing my backpack on my lap. Epp puts his suitcase behind the seat.

We're moving. My excitement builds as the truck pulls away from the restaurant and away from the police who are looking for me. The next time we stop, we'll be in Monroeville.

Epp leans over and whispers in my ear. "Tell me what happened out there." Epp's voice has a stern quality. It sounds surprisingly like my father's.

"I got us a lift," I reply.

Epp frowns. He takes out the atlas from his coat pocket and opens it to the state of Alabama, intent on charting our trip to Monroeville.

I shift my backpack and relax.

"Where you from?" the driver asks me.

"Minnesota."

He reaches into his shirt pocket and takes out a cigarette and lighter. "That explains the accent. You ever been south before?" He sticks the cigarette between his lips and flicks the lighter once, producing a small flame. I hold my breath as he inhales deeply.

"No."

"Did you hitchhike all the way down here?"

I shift uncomfortably, wishing he didn't ask so many questions. "We took the bus, but our tickets ran out at Montgomery."

"You rode the dogs all the way down here, huh? What are you going to Monroeville for?" I glance at Epp, who didn't hear him because he's watching the traffic on the interstate, which is surprisingly busy at this early hour. We're sitting high above the cars. The sun is peeking out through a light haze.

"To find my mom," I say, and it isn't entirely a lie.

Chapter Twenty-three

South on Interstate 65
March 15, 1986, 8:30 a.m.

I read somewhere
that all fiction is based on personal experience.
That no matter what we write
we're really writing about ourselves.
That would explain why
Harper Lee is such a mystery.

I'm jolted awake when the rig turns off the road into a gas station. I open my eyes, squinting through the smoke-filled cab. "Is this Monroeville?"

"Yep. The outskirts. The center of town is a few miles that way." He points but I don't catch the direction. "I need fuel and I can't afford any more time out of my schedule. Maybe you can walk or find another ride in."

I nudge Epp, who's asleep, his head resting on the jacket that's propped against the window.

"Epp, wake up. We have to get out."

We're left standing in the bright sunlight, our coats thrown over our shoulders and our bags in hand. Epp is still bleary-eyed; his forehead has the imprint of a button in it.

"Maybe if we'd been better company, the driver would have taken us into town," Epp says as he shakes his head. We enter the gas station to use the restroom. The smell of coffee and sausage drifts from a small diner tucked on the side.

In the bathroom, I put on a clean shirt and jeans. I also brush my teeth. I don't want to have dragon breath when I meet Harper Lee.

I return to find Epp staring at a map of Monroeville near the front of the gas station. His face is clean shaven, but he's wearing the same smelly flannel shirt. He's frowning. "We have about a five-mile walk."

"Let's get going," I say enthusiastically.

Epp looks down at his suitcase, and I can tell he doesn't like the idea of dragging that behind him. "Maybe I can get us a ride. I'll check around. You wait here."

I wait near the door. Ten minutes later I'm still waiting, staring at the passing cars. Finally, Epp returns.

"If we're willing to wait about a half hour, there's a couple going downtown who will give us a ride."

"A half hour!" My voice sounds whiny, much like I feel right now.

Epp pats me on the shoulder. "Hang in there. We'll make it."

I grunt and drop my stuff onto the floor. "I don't know, Epp. Seems like there's always something going wrong."

Epp inspects the candy aisle. "You're just having second thoughts."

I follow him to the candy aisle. "What if I've changed my mind about seeing Harper Lee?"

Epp turns to face me. "That's your nerves talking, Erin. You'd regret it if you didn't try."

I run my fingers through my hair. "I know."

Epp buys two Snickers and a bag of M&M's. I buy some breath mints in case the brushing wasn't enough.

The elderly couple take their sweet time, but we're soon on the road, headed toward town in the back seat of their Pontiac Bonneville.

We pass several trees with white blossoms.

"What kind of trees are those?" I ask.

"Those are magnolias," the man replies, and the word *magnolia* rolls off his tongue with a hint of reverence.

"Doesn't Harper Lee live in this town?" Epp asks as he winks at me.

The man nods. "She sure does."

The man's wife turns toward the back. "Are you fans of hers?"

"I can get extra credit in English if I bring back some information about her," I say nonchalantly.

Her husband glances at me in the rearview mirror. "Then you should visit the museum. You'll find lots of information there."

He drives us to the center of town, right in front of an old building set in the town square. Bushes covered with flowers fill the lawn.

"The museum is on the top floor of the old courthouse," the man says and smiles. "Have fun."

We thank them for the ride and are left staring up at a red brick building. The side is framed by a porch with stone steps. The top of the building is white, and it has a large round clock in the middle. The building sits south of a newer courthouse. Surrounding the square are small stores, a post office, a bank, and a friendly looking café.

A gentle breeze washes over us.

"It's perfect, just like I imagined it would be."

Epp gives the building a once-over. "Let's go inside."

"Sure."

Epp pulls his suitcase behind him. "I wish we blended in more."

Several men wearing overalls are busy trimming the evergreen shrubs along the side of the courthouse.

Epp eyes the bushes and the workers, then shakes the idea out of his head. "It's a museum. They're used to tourists."

Our shoes echo as we walk into the courtroom, a large, empty room filled with windows that flood the floor with sunlight. At the far end, in the center, the judge's stand is positioned with an American flag on one side and an Alabama state flag on the other. A Bible and gavel sit on the judge's bench.

We leave our stuff at the door and walk toward the judge's stand. A churchlike atmosphere fills the room. Along the upper wall, a balcony frames the sides and back. This is just like the courtroom described in *Mockingbird.*

"No wonder she used this as a model," Epp finally says, and I wonder if he's reading my mind. "This place rings with inspiration." We stand for several minutes before Epp takes out a small camera and flashes several pictures.

"Go ahead. Sit at the judge's bench," he tells me. "I'll take your picture."

I sit down at the bench, feeling like a pilgrim on hallowed ground. "So this is what it feels like," I whisper to myself.

We spend another fifteen minutes looking around the courtroom. I want to climb the stairs to the balcony, but it's closed.

I imagine the people who once filled this space: Harper Lee's father, who practiced law here; Harper Lee and her friend Truman Capote, who watched from the balcony above. The people change in my mind, and Scout and her friend Dill are now watching as Scout's father, Atticus, below them, defends Tom Robinson in front of a packed courtroom. I know one image is real and one is fictional, but the line seems hazy at this moment.

Epp steers me toward the museum, where we're greeted by a friendly woman who is busily sorting through photos and postcards. A mug of steaming coffee sits to the side of a small register. There are color prints of the courthouse and a twentieth-anniversary edition of *To Kill a Mockingbird*, as well as numerous books by Truman Capote. A large picture of Harper Lee hangs on the wall. Another wall shows an old map of Monroeville.

I'm staring at the memorabilia, wishing I had money to spend, when Epp asks the woman if she knows where Harper Lee lives.

"I'm not sure she's in town right now. She doesn't usually like to be disturbed," the woman replies. "She's very private."

Epp shrugs and thanks her anyway, then buys a postcard.

I grab him as soon as we get outside. "What are we going to do? Walk down every street looking for Harper Lee's house?"

Epp ignores my concerns, showing me his post-card, a picture of the outside of the museum, which he plans to send to his mom back in Missouri.

"Let's try that place," he says and steps off the curb

into the middle of the street as he heads toward a small drugstore. He enters and I slowly follow, then head to the bathroom.

When I return, Epp is already on a first-name basis with the man at the counter. Epp puts his hand on my shoulder.

"Erin traveled all the way from Minnesota just to get a look at Harper Lee's house. We've already visited the courthouse, so we thought we'd mosey on over past her house and enjoy the scenery. It's three blocks down that way, right?" Epp points vaguely west.

The man shakes his head. "No, it's that way." He points in the opposite direction. "Two blocks down and to the left. Middle of the block on the left side, with black trim. Can't miss it."

"Right." Epp nods as if he knew it all along. Then he buys a candy bar for the walk.

Outside, I hug him. "You did it, Epp!"

He takes the wrapper off the candy bar. "Now comes the hard part. You going through with this?"

It's a good question. Will I have the guts to actually do it? I take a deep breath. "I didn't come all this way to just walk past her house."

"Okay, then." He leads me down the street,

pulling his green suitcase behind him. He stops to take a picture of a tree with pink tuliplike blooms.

My heart pounds louder with each passing block. We walk faster now. We're on a mission. If I wasn't so nervous I'd enjoy the moment, but I'm scared to death. That she won't be home. That she will be home.

I notice the flowers and green grass, things I haven't seen for six months in Minnesota, as I follow Epp down the sidewalk. Epp stops in front of a simple brick ranch-style house on a small hill near a school. It looks smaller than my house in St. Paul. No huge Southern homestead like I'd expected. No big trees or wraparound porch.

"This is it," he says with certainty. The mailbox has the name Lee painted in black letters.

I take out my mother's diary. I'm not sure my legs work, but I make it to the door. Epp is still on the street out front. I turn and knock lightly. I thought I would be overcome with joy at this point—I'm finally here—but something doesn't seem quite right. I clutch the diary in my hand, my fingers pinching the marked page, afraid it will disappear if I let go of my tight grip. Nothing happens. I knock again, this time loudly. Nothing. I turn toward Epp, who shrugs.

"She has to be home," I yell, knocking even harder. No one answers. I peek in a window but can't see much through the curtain. I'm so upset I start pounding the door hard.

"Stop!" Epp grabs me from behind.

"It's all wrong. This isn't how it's supposed to be."

Chapter Twenty-four

Harper Lee's House
March 15, 1986, 11:30 a.m.

"It isn't fair." I lean my head against the door and sob. "I traveled thirteen hundred miles. She should have been home."

"She'll be back later," Epp says encouragingly.

A neighbor peeks out her window and I back away from the house. "What if she's out of town?"

Epp looks around uncomfortably. "I don't know. You can't hang around here until she returns."

I take an envelope from my backpack. It was a last-minute thought in case I chickened out. I write "Harper Lee" across the front and put my return address in the corner. Then I choose two of my stories and stick them inside the envelope.

"Are you going to leave a note?" Epp asks.

I nod. Ripping out a page from my journal, I scribble a quick message before I change my mind.

Dear Miss Lee,

Sorry I missed you. I wanted to talk to you about my mom. Her name was Kate Kampbell. She wrote you a letter in 1963. Like my mom, I also want to be a writer. I hope you enjoy my stories.

Sincerely,
Erin Garven

I walk to the mailbox and put the letter inside.

"It isn't supposed to end this way," I say bitterly.

Epp glances at the house. "Hey, it's not over yet. We'll come back later." We both stare at the house, as if we're waiting for something to happen.

Epp takes out his camera and flashes two pictures. The neighbor is now staring at us through the window.

"I'm hungry," I say. "Let's find someplace to eat."

We walk back to the center of town and find a restaurant that specializes in Southern cooking.

I spot a gas station phone booth, but my stomach is growling. The call has waited this long—it can wait until after lunch.

"You have any money left?" Epp asks as we walk toward the parking lot. It's hot out now. He wipes sweat off his face with his sleeve.

I check my purse. Five dollars and some change. How can I survive on that amount?

"I have some," I say. Maybe I can get an order of fries.

The place is bustling. It's not well lit, but the coolness of the dark interior feels good. We're seated in a booth near the window. Epp tucks his suitcase under the booth. I throw my backpack on the seat next to me and sink down into the soft red vinyl. We're given two menus and glasses of water. An order of biscuits and gravy is only $3.75. I don't have to starve after all.

A pretty waitress gives me a nod as she passes our booth and hurries toward two older women at the table next to us. The waitress balances three dishes in her hands.

"Here you are, Alice and Nelle. The usual."

I turn my attention to Epp and put down my menu. "I'm not going back to her house."

Epp almost drops his menu. "But we're in Monroeville."

"I know. I'm sorry I went berserk on you." I shrug and fetch up a long sigh. "But I don't feel so bad anymore. Why is that?"

Epp smiles. "You made it. You completed your pilgrimage."

"That *Wizard of Oz* kind of thing?"

"If you want to get philosophical on me, yes."

I imagine Epp as the lion, the tin man, and the scarecrow rolled into one.

"I thought I was just cracking up from lack of sleep."

He nods. "That too. Are you going to call your dad after we eat?"

"Yes." I wince at the thought of facing Dad. I know I deserve whatever punishment he gives. But I hope he understands my reasons for coming here. I hope he doesn't ground me for the rest of my high school life.

"Well, what have you learned, Dorothy?" Epp lets out a small laugh.

I pick up my book. "*Mockingbird* led me to my mom. But thinking that Harper Lee is a magical link to Mom is stupid. Her diary means so much more to me than meeting Harper Lee. Why did it take me thirty hours on a bus to realize that?"

"All right!" Epp pounds his fist on the table, startling the two women across from us, then says softly, "You won't be too disappointed, then, if you don't meet her?"

I pause for a moment. "I left her a note. That's good enough."

Epp seems satisfied. "You can click your heels now."

"If only it were that easy," I say.

When the waitress returns, Epp orders the house special, catfish with biscuits and gravy, an order of grits, and a large Coke. I order biscuits and gravy and ask for more water.

"Where are you headed after this?" I ask Epp when the waitress leaves.

"Thought I'd head to Infocom."

"Really? Are you going to show them your game?"

Epp shrugs. "Maybe when I finish it. I just want to visit their headquarters."

I nod.

"You going to be okay? With the new mom and going back to high school and all?"

"Probably," I admit, although I'm not entirely convinced.

Epp brings his hands together. "You know, just because your mom isn't living in this world doesn't mean she has to be dead to you. I talk to my dad all the time. I have a feeling he's listening."

A waft of cinnamon floats up from the table next to us. "I don't know. I wish there was another way to tell her how I feel."

Epp shakes his head and two red curls fly up. "You'll figure it out, Erin. I'm sure of that."

"Thanks for all your help, for everything." I think of how inadequate that sounds after all he's done for me. Jeff and Bruce could take lessons from him.

He brushes off my thank-you as if it's unnecessary. "You owe me a copy of your first book."

I imagine my name on the cover of a novel. "Agreed."

Epp excuses himself to use the restroom. I stare out the window, wondering how I'm going to explain any of this to Amy. I'm already a nerd at school. What will happen when everyone hears about me running away to meet Harper Lee? And then I didn't even talk to her.

I open my journal and start writing. I describe the restaurant we're in and the two women sitting across from us, one, white-haired with a cane resting near her chair, the other, younger, with dark and gray-flecked hair, sipping coffee. I describe the singing sound of spatulas in the kitchen flipping an order of catfish on the grill and the heavenly aroma of freshly baked biscuits.

The two women stare at me. Do I look a mess? Is it obvious I'm a runaway?

The dark-haired woman glances at *Mockingbird* sitting on the edge of the table, then winks at me. The older woman says, "Good book," and smiles.

"It is," I agree. "My favorite."

They return to their meals. I shift in my seat, then look down again at my journal.

The waitress brings silverwave. "Are you a reporter?" she asks in a friendly voice. Her nametag reads "Sherri."

"No," I answer, a bit flustered, but flattered that she would think so. "I'm visiting. Trying to capture the feel of the place while it's still fresh in my mind."

"So you're a writer?" It's as if she's trying to figure me out.

"No," I begin, then stop. What was it that woman on the bus said? I clear my throat and state firmly, "Yes, I'm a writer. I just haven't been published yet."

Sherri nods. "Well, you're in the right place. The literary capital of the South. Your food is just about up."

I take a sip of water and turn back to my journal. The two women are speaking in low voices. The waitress brings our food, and I inhale the smell before plunging in with my fork. Epp arrives as the women are leaving. They nod at me and smile.

Epp delves into the first of his waiting plates of food. I try a bite of his grits before deciding I'm not suited to the exotic tastes of Southern cooking.

Sherri brings our check and Epp grabs it. "This one is on me," he says in an unyielding voice. I don't argue.

"By the way," Sherri says as she turns to clean off the other table, "Nelle and Alice had a suggestion for you. They overheard you two talking, and said that you should write your mother a letter." She pauses and wrinkles her nose. "Does that make any sense?"

I'm embarrassed that these women heard me talk about my problems. But a letter actually makes sense. "Thanks," I say, and smile.

"You're welcome," Sherri says, then returns to her chore.

"A letter is a good idea. I don't know why I didn't think of it before," I tell Epp.

He bobs his head in agreement, his mouth full. We finish eating while I think of where to begin. How do I write to my mom after sixteen years?

"Do you want to call home now?" Epp asks when we finish eating.

"Sure."

"I'll go pay the bill," Epp says.

I look out the window. My first trip south and all I can do is worry. I wish Dad were here now and not angry with me. I crave my boring life again, complete with my brothers and Susan.

I'm not sure if it's sheer exhaustion or my mind playing tricks on me, but I think I see Dad. I mean *really* see Dad! At least it looks like Dad pumping gas into a Buick at the station across the street. It can't be him, of course. That's not our car. It has Alabama license plates.

The man stares absently at the restaurant. He has the same lanky build and dark hair as Dad. He even stands the same way, shoulders up and slightly forward. He's staring at me, although he doesn't see me.

I gasp. It is Dad!

How did he find me?

He looks tired and has a pained expression.

I'm responsible for that look.

Chapter Twenty-five

Monroeville, Alabama
March 15, 1986, 2:00 p.m.

I thought my life was awful,
or maybe I willed it so,
but nothing's as bad
as we make it out to be.
Like a dull, gray March sky,
the sun will, sooner or later,
find a way to peek through.

I find my feet and walk up to the checkout counter, where Epp is complimenting Sherri on the best cat-fish he's ever tasted.

"Epp, you won't believe this," I whisper. "My dad's outside. I just saw him at the gas station across the street."

"You're kidding!" Epp turns to look.

I shake my head. "What am I going to tell him? That I ran away to find Harper Lee but then when I got here she wasn't home so I decided I didn't want to meet her after all? He'll think I'm nuts."

Sherri hands Epp his change. "What do you mean?" she says. "Weren't you talking to Miss Lee and her sister a few minutes ago?"

"Harper Lee, the author?" I ask, as if there's more than one in town.

"Miss Nelle Harper Lee. We call her Nelle. One and the same. She comes here almost every day with her sister."

Epp starts laughing and slaps me on the back. "You met her and you didn't even know it!"

"How stupid of me. No wonder she stared at my book. How could I not have remembered that her name is Nelle!"

"Well, she doesn't like to be fussed over," Sherri assures us.

Epp looks outside. "Your dad is going to his car. You'd better hurry, Erin."

"Oh, right. Good-bye, Sherri, and thanks," I say as I turn to run. "You'll come meet my dad, won't you, Epp?"

He nods. "In a few minutes."

I run out of the restaurant and across the street.

"Dad. Wait!"

He peers over the top of the car, squinting as if he doesn't quite believe what he's seeing. Then a look of relief crosses his face. If I ever had doubt of it before, the certainty now shines plainly in his eyes.

"You came," I say.

Dad throws his arms around me and gathers me close.

"Thank God," he says in a whisper. My face feels wet. I'm not sure if it's from my tears or Dad's or a mixture of the two. He pulls me back. "Are you all right?"

I try to answer, but my voice is trapped inside a sob.

He gently shakes me. "I was so worried, Erin."

I can only whisper, "I know."

Then I bury my face in his shirt. I feel the knot in my stomach loosen, then slip away. Right now that seems to be enough.

Chapter Twenty-six

"How did you find me?"

Dad's eyes narrow. "I had a pretty good idea who you wanted to visit. Then I got a phone call from a woman in Kansas City. She said she was a friend of yours from the bus."

"Sedushia?"

"I think that was her name. She told me where you were going. So I booked the next flight to Montgomery and rented a car there. I prayed all the way."

I stare at a dirty candy wrapper on the ground, avoiding Dad's eyes. "I'm sorry, Dad. I shouldn't have left like that."

His voice above me is sad. "I didn't think things were that bad between us."

"They aren't," I try to reassure him, my eyes filling

up again. "I just thought they were. Everything is changing so fast."

He places his hand on the back of my head. "You don't have to tell me that. You're almost all grown up."

That wasn't the change I was thinking of, but it doesn't matter right now. Dad looks past me at Epp, who's standing so quietly behind me that I didn't know he was there.

I quickly wipe my eyes. "This is Epp, a friend from the bus. He helped me get here and made sure I called home."

"Nice to meet you, Epp." Dad shakes Epp's hand like they're old friends. Then Dad turns to me. "Sounds like you got to know several people on your trip."

"Yeah," I say, not knowing where to begin.

Dad's eyes are penetrating. "We need to work out a few things between us."

I let out a quick breath before I say it. "I want to know more about Mom."

Dad seems puzzled. He scratches at his chin, now thick with fuzz. "What do you want to know?"

I shift my weight and stand up straight. "Everything."

Dad rubs his temple as if he's thinking it over. "I'll

make you a deal. I'll tell you whatever you want to know. But not until we get some rest."

The biscuits and gravy are weighing heavy in my stomach. "Sounds good to me."

"And no more running away," he adds, looking at Epp.

Dad drives us to the Best Western and pays for two rooms, even though Epp objects.

After Dad calls Susan and Bruce and Jeff, he seems to collapse from fatigue. I watch him sleep, his arm drawn up underneath the pillow. I guess it's not so bad that Dad's marrying Susan. It might be nice to have another woman in the house.

I worry he won't remember.
It's been sixteen years
since she died.
What if she's too dim a memory?

I relax on my bed with a list of questions, everything from Mom's favorite color to her favorite singer.

There's one question I'm saving till last. It's the most important question of all: Why didn't you ever talk about Mom?

Chapter Twenty-seven

March 16, 1986, 10:00 a.m.

*I've decided that real life
is better than fiction.
Real life is a family that loves me.*

We left Monroeville this morning. It could have been Maycomb, the town in *Mockingbird*, a long time ago, but it's different now. A Winn-Dixie grocery store sits off Alabama Avenue, and modern businesses line the streets. A stone wall is all that remains of Harper Lee's old neighborhood.

Dad pulls up in front of the Montgomery bus terminal to let Epp out.

"Thanks, Mr. Garven. Thanks for the room and the ride."

"The pleasure is all mine. Thank you for taking care of my girl."

Epp shakes Dad's hand and gets out.

I open the car door and follow.

I reach over and give Epp a hug. "I'll miss you." He blushes and hands me a piece of paper filled with names and addresses.

"What's this?"

"A list of people from the bus. In case you ever want to write to any of us."

"Thanks. I'll be sure to write. Do you have my address?"

Epp flashes one of my dad's business cards that has our home address. He tucks it into his shirt pocket as they announce boarding for his bus.

"Take care, Erin. I'll send you the pictures I took." He glances at the waiting bus. "Thanks for letting me share your adventure. You've inspired me."

Then he turns to go. It's the same as it was with Sedushia, this feeling that I'm leaving someone special.

"I want to hear about the rest of your trip," I yell at him and he waves back. His flannel shirt blends into the crowd and my stomach tenses.

Dad honks the horn and I get back in.

"Are you going to tell me about your trip?"

I nod and take out my list of questions. "But you're first," I say before I lose my nerve.

He pulls the Buick away from the curb and heads out toward the interstate. We pass Pancake Heaven. Two officers sit in the window booth, drinking coffee.

Dad shifts nervously in his seat. I'm tempted to make small talk. But I don't say anything. I'm anxious to hear about Mom.

Dad clears his throat and stares at the highway. "I never intended it to be this way. It was just too hard to talk about her. I thought it'd get easier with time." He turns to look at me. "It didn't."

His voice is sad. I stare at the list of questions in front of me.

"When I met Susan, things changed. I fell in love again, when I didn't think I ever would. It doesn't seem as hard now to talk about your mom."

We come to a stoplight and Dad reaches over and squeezes my shoulder. "So fire away," he says, and his voice is lighter.

"You sure?" I ask.

"Absolutely."

"Okay." I settle into my seat. "First question. Why didn't you tell me Mom wanted to be a writer?"

Dad shrugs. "Kate wanted to write, but she wanted to be a mother even more. She didn't talk about it much. Our lives were pretty full back then.

I'd just started with the station, we'd bought our first house, and Jeff and Bruce were little. I think she might have gone back to it when you kids got older."

Dad and I talk all the way to the airport and during the entire flight home. We talk mostly about Mom, and Susan, too. Our mouths ache from all the back and forth.

It's evening by the time we pull into our driveway. As soon as we walk into the house, Bruce rushes over and hugs me. "Don't scare us like that again," he scolds when he lets me go.

"I won't." I take a step back, uncomfortable with the attention. "I'm going to put my stuff away."

Jeff waves as I go to my room. "Welcome back," he says. "I took care of your cat. She spent most of the time under your bed. I think she missed you."

He flashes me a weak smile. "Me, too," he says, and I smile back.

It feels good to be home.

Chapter Twenty-eight

Central High School, St. Paul, Minnesota
March 28, 1986, 2:00 p.m.

Susan asked me to be a junior bridesmaid.
I said yes.

I enter the college counselor's office, a cramped room with half-hidden posters plastered on the walls between shelves that are stacked with books and school paraphernalia. The bell rings for seventh period the day before Easter break. Everyone's leaving early. It's been two weeks since my trip south. I haven't told anyone about my chance encounter with Harper Lee, not even Dad or Amy. They'd act excited if I told them, but I'm not sure they'd understand. I don't think anyone except Mom could relate to the experience. I'll never know if Harper Lee ever wrote back to her, but I'd like to think she did. There are a few dusty boxes in the attic I haven't opened. Dad said one of them is Mom's.

I skim through several college brochures, searching for one with a good writing program. Dad and I have been talking more. High school seemed like it would last forever, but Jeff is graduating in two months, and next year I'll be a junior.

"I can't believe you went to Alabama all by yourself," Amy said when I told her about my trip. She acted impressed and insisted that next time I take her along.

I think about high school. Dad said I should make the most of these years. I've signed up to work on the school newspaper. They asked me to write book reviews. I'm going to start with *Mockingbird*.

It's dusk when our family attends Good Friday services at St. Agnes Church, as we do every year. This is the church where Dad and Susan will be married in June. I sit next to Dad in the front row as the priest talks of death and resurrection and starting anew, like the green buds on the ash tree outside the church. Father McGuire looks down at me and I remember the magnolia trees and how alive I'd felt standing in front of the Monroeville Courthouse Museum.

Maybe because I'd just finished reading Mom's diary, or maybe because I know she would have felt the same way.

After church we go to the Knights of Columbus fish fry because Dad volunteered to work. Dad takes off his jacket and rolls up the sleeves of his white shirt as he prepares to take over as server. They're short on help. Dad looks at me, winks, and points to an apron.

"Come on." I grab Jeff's arm. "Time to put that free-throw shooting arm to work."

Pretty soon all five of us are pitching in, clearing off tables, carrying pans from the kitchen, and pouring steaming cups of coffee. The place is crowded, and the line waiting to eat stretches out the front door.

An older woman with white hair tied up in a bun holds on to a walker while trying to balance her plate as she stands in line. She grimaces from the effort. I offer to carry her plate to the table.

"Thank you, dear."

When I fill her coffee cup she pats me on the arm. "You are so much like your father." She smiles and sits down.

Later, Jeff and I are working the same table; he's clearing off and I'm setting up clean silverware and cups.

"Don't get the wrong idea," he says as he holds a dirty plate in his hands. "I mean, I still think you're psycho, but you had a lot of guts to go all the way to Alabama to visit your hero. Too bad you didn't meet her."

I keep working. "Who says I didn't meet her?"

Jeff looks at me as if he can't decide whether I'm lying. He shakes his head. "You were definitely adopted."

We work for two hours before the crowd lessens and we get a chance to sit down and eat. Everything smells fishy, even my new blouse. We're all sweaty, but hard work can make even a piece of breaded cod and runny coleslaw appetizing. I look up from my plate and catch Dad gazing at Susan. His eyes beam with affection, and I know this is the way things are supposed to be.

"Anyone for dessert?" Dad looks toward the cake table.

"Sure. Go for it," I reply. Susan smiles at me and I smile back.

Dear Mom,

Harper Lee once wrote, "As one holds down a cork to the bottom of a stream, so may love be imprisoned by self." I feel like I've become uncorked and let loose with a flood of feelings I didn't even know I had. Your diary was the best gift I'll ever receive. Dad says I remind him of you. Now that I've gotten to know you, I think you would have liked Susan. She's not so bad, after all. I'll be off to college in a couple of years and Dad will need someone. It's good he has Susan. I guess that's a start.

Thanks for sending me on a journey I'll never forget. I'll write again later.

Love,
Erin

Thank you to the following:

Jane Resh-Thomas and my writing groups; Christy Ottaviano; Jennifer Flannery; Jim Ellsworth, computer genius, for the great bookmarks; student editors Deanna Anderson, Elle Bowman, Katie Broadwell, Samantha Olsen, and Debra Molstad; Monica Barnes, who traveled with me to Monroeville, Alabama; the residents of Monroeville, Alabama, who showed us what Southern hospitality is all about.

And a special thank-you to Harper Lee for inspiring writers to strive for what she's already attained: perfection.

42421778R00121

Made in the USA
Lexington, KY
21 June 2015